ALSO, BY BRYAN WEMPEN

Fiction:

Adoption, Inc.: A Family Affair (2025)

In Albuquerque's heat and a junkyard full of dreams, the Trenton family tries to build a future through unconventional adoptions and risky schemes. But as ambition collides with desperation, love, loyalty, and survival hang in the balance—forcing one family to confront how far they'll go to hold themselves together.

Unbound Ambitions: The Candidate (2025)

In New Mexico and Washington, D.C., rival campaigns collide over truth, power, and redemption. As secrets unravel, one idealistic team must confront corruption's cost to reclaim democracy—or lose the nation's soul.

Sumner Whispers, A Wyoming Murder Mystery of Secrets, Shadows, and Cursed Legacies (The Wyoming Murder Mysteries Series, 2024)

Secrets lurk beneath the surface in the quiet town of Sumner, Wyoming. Sheriff Grace Thompson must uncover the truth behind a shocking murder that ties the town's dark past to a chilling new crime.

Non-Fiction:

F**K My Demons: Redefining Normal (2024)

Personal Transformation – An honest and bold exploration of overcoming personal demons and rediscovering spirit and purpose in life, blending personal stories with powerful personal growth messages.

Sober Is Better: My Note to Self (2019)

Memoir & Addiction Recovery – A raw and personal account of Bryan's journey through addiction and recovery, offering hope and lessons learned along the way.

Note to Self: A Collection of 99 Life Lessons (2015)

Self-Improvement – An inspirational collection of personal reflections and lessons learned throughout life, offering practical advice and insights on growth, resilience, and mindfulness.

Dancing with Big Data (2015)

Technology & Business – A thought-provoking exploration of how big data is transforming industries and reshaping decision-making, featuring insights from leading experts on the future of data in business.

DRINK
SOME FIGHTS ARE WORTH THE SCARS

BRYAN WEMPEN

A SHORT NOVEL

Published by Red Yarrow Books
Santa Fe, New Mexico

BRYAN WEMPEN

Published by Red Yarrow Books,
an imprint of Cerrillos Road Holdings. Santa Fe, New Mexico

Red Yarrow Books are available at special discounts for events,
promotions, fundraising, or educational purposes when purchased in bulk.
For details, please get in touch with us at
redyarrowbooks@cerrillosroad.com

Cover design — Sherwin Emmanuel Minhas
Bio photo — Michella Wempen

Library of Congress Control Number: 2025946801
ISBN: 979-8-9887219-8-7
eISBN: 979-8-9887219-9-4

Printed in the United States of America
Published in the City of Santa Fe, New Mexico

To Ernest Hemingway:
I've read your work and taken some time to reflect on it. In many ways, I've experienced the very struggles, silences, and search for meaning that you've so eloquently expressed.

Now, I write in what is known as a style you helped shape—one you architected with precision and a particular type of courage. You weren't perfect in life by all accounts—none of us are.

But your writing was damn close.

DRINK

SOME FIGHTS ARE WORTH THE SCARS

CHAPTER ONE

He woke up in a stranger's bed with the sun punching through a crooked window and his tongue thick as bread dough. The girl beside him had short, dark hair and one eye open, watching him as if he owed her something.

He probably did.

There was a taste in his mouth like pennies and regret. He didn't remember her name but he knew she had called him charming. He usually was—especially when he wasn't trying. That's how the night had gone. He'd said something funny. Then something sad. Then something mean. Then something sad, again. Then she took his hand.

Dressing quietly, she didn't stop him. Didn't ask him to stay. There was no pretend breakfast offer. No talk of texting or trying again. Just the long silence of mutual understanding.

He walked the few blocks back to his apartment in the old part of the city—stucco peeling. Mailbox leaning. The kind of place where windows were stuck and neighbors didn't ask questions. His key stuck.

His head throbbed.

Inside, he drank warm water from the tap and opened the cabinet above the fridge. Three bottles. He picked one, unscrewed the cap, and poured half into a coffee mug that said "World's Best Uncle." He didn't have any nieces or nephews.

He sat at the kitchen table and stared at the wall. The light came in sideways, an orange, dusty glow. It lit up the water stains on the ceiling like halos.

He had once been a teacher. Literature. **Sophocles. Baldwin. Quinones. Twain.** He'd loved it until he didn't. Until his hands shook and the principal spoke slowly and carefully, like he was breaking up with someone. They called it a leave of absence.

It is freedom for him. Then called it something else. Then stopped calling it anything.

The mug was empty. He filled it again.

By noon, he had showered, shaved, and put on a clean shirt. He had somewhere to be. A meeting with a woman named Clare, who ran a school that took second chances seriously. She'd found his resume on some old website and said she liked the way he phrased things.

He was good at phrasing things. Not so good at finishing them.

Outside, the sky was blue enough to make him nervous. Too blue. Too honest. He put on sunglasses even though it wasn't that bright.

At the corner, he passed a man selling tamales and burritos, and smiled at the way the guy counted change as if it mattered. He envied that—small math. Straight lines.

Clare met him at a café that smelled like cardamom and decaf. She was tall, blunt, and kind-eyed. Wore her hair short like she was all business and had no time for nonsense.

"You still want to teach?" she asked.

Avery shrugged. "Sometimes I even want to fly."

She didn't smile. "You still drink?"

He thought of lying, then didn't. "Less."

"That's not a no."

He tapped his fingers on the mug. "That's not a yes either."

"You'd be working with high schoolers. You'd need to be clean."

He nodded. "I know."

There was a pause, like a door between them that neither wanted to open too fast.

"You've got the brains for it," she said. "But I need to know you're not going to fall apart."

He gave her a look that had won bar wagers and defused fights. That lopsided grin that said *I'm fine, but not really. But maybe.*

"I fall apart quietly," he said. "And never in front of children."

She didn't laugh, but she didn't leave.

He walked home with a folded piece of paper in his pocket—start date, temporary contract. Two weeks out.

There was time. He had time to dry out. He had to be better. He constantly told himself that very thing.

That night, he poured another drink and raised the mug to no one.

"Here's to time," he said. And drank.

CHAPTER TWO

That's what he did when he didn't want to drink, didn't want to sit, and didn't want to sleep. The city was too hot for jackets, but he wore one anyway. The sleeves were long, and the pockets were deep, and that made him feel safe.

Avery Sloan. Thirty-three. Too smart for his own good and not smart enough to stop proving it to the world and himself. A man with a head full of poems and hands that shook when no one was looking.

He passed a record shop, a closed diner, and a building with windows all papered over. The wind smelled like hot asphalt and yesterday's tortillas. He used to love this part of the city. The grit of it. The honesty. Now it just reminded him of how long he'd been walking in circles.

There was a time when he had answers for everything. That was before he knew better. Before he learned that being right didn't mean you were okay. People didn't stick around just because you could quote Bukowski and Camus or get drunk with style.

He crossed into the park, sat on a bench that baked in the sun, watching an old man feed crows and pigeons. Watched a boy fall off a skateboard and get up without crying. That part impressed him. The not-crying.

A group of teenagers walked past. Loud. Alive. One of them wore a shirt with a quote he used to teach: *"So it goes."* He smiled. That book had gotten him through a winter once. Maybe a couple of seasons.

His mind wandered again. To a classroom. A chalkboard. A kid with no jacket, biting his nails, always asking questions that didn't have answers. He wondered where that kid ended up. Prison maybe. Or worse—selling insurance.

He leaned back. Closed his eyes. Thought about not thinking.

He was somewhere in the middle of a sentence he wasn't saying when he heard it:

"Avery."

It came sharply. Familiar. A woman's voice. Not angry, not soft. Just enough steel to cut through the fog.

He opened his eyes and blinked. "Nico." He said.

Nico Hart, the only person who hadn't given up on him entirely. Social worker. Smart. Used to be a poet. Gave it up for something more useful. They'd gone to school together once and slept together once. Fought like war veterans and laughed like drunk saints.

Now she stood in front of him, one hand on her hip, the other holding a takeout cup. Her hair was tied up with a pencil. She wore scuffed boots and a face that didn't forgive much.

"You're doing it again," she said.

He squinted. "Sitting?"

"Falling into your own head."

"Better than falling into traffic."

She didn't laugh. She sat down beside him and handed him the cup. It was coffee. Good coffee.

He sipped. "You always know what crack to find me."

"I always know where lost things end up."

They sat in silence. Ravens fought over crumbs. A baby screamed in the distance. A wind came up and left just as quickly.

"I got a job," he said finally.

She nodded, slowly. "I heard. Clare called me."

"You two friends?"

"We circle each other over the years."

"I'll drink to that," he said, then flinched. "Sorry, not funny, I suppose."

"It's fine," she said, and it wasn't. "You going to take it seriously this time?"

"I want to."

"That's not the same."

He didn't answer.

After a while, she stood up and looked down at him. "Don't screw it up, Ave."

"Trying not to."

She paused. "Trying isn't enough." Then she walked off. Just like that. Like it was all she had time for. Like maybe she knew he wouldn't follow. And he didn't.

He sat there until the cup was empty and the ravens were gone, and as the sun began to dip, it revealed a pink and orange New Mexico sky—a sight Avery had stopped noticing long ago.

Then he stood. Put the cup in the trash. Adjusted his coat like it meant something.

And walked.

CHAPTER THREE

Mr. Optimistic always thought to himself that the school smelled of body odor, sanitizer, and below-average ambition—even on its best days. The floor wax never seemed to dry completely, and the lights hummed overhead as if they were nervous.

Avery stood in the doorway of Room 112, gripping a cheap red pen like it was a cigarette. The desk had his name on it—**Mr. Sloan**—written on a laminated sign someone had printed and forgotten about. He touched it once, like it might vanish if he stared too long.

Kids shuffled in. High school juniors. Tired faces, backpacks slung low, earbuds still in. They looked through him as if he were an outdated app.

He understood that.

He cleared his throat. No one looked up.

"Phones away," he said, voice even.

Nothing happened. One kid snorted.

"Now," he added.

That got their attention.

A few eye-rolls, a couple of sighs—but they complied. A small victory, he thought.

He wrote his name on the board. **Sloan, Avery.** He liked how clean it looked in Expo black. He liked that it didn't say "alcoholic" or "washout."

"You're stuck with me for the semester," he said. "Don't worry. I'm probably just as disappointed as you are."

A girl laughed, one bark of amusement. The kind that slips out before you remember you're supposed to be cool.

He liked her immediately.

"We'll read books," he said. "You'll write things. I'll grade them. Or I won't. Sometimes the system eats homework and sometimes I forget. Either way, everyone gets a little closer to graduation."

A boy in the back raised a hand. He had headphones hanging from his neck and a skateboard clipped to his bag.

"You gonna be, like, chill?"

Avery shrugged. "That depends. Are you gonna be, like, awake?"

A few more laughs this time. He let them settle.

"Let's start with names," he said. "Just first names. Nothing fancy. You're not auditioning for Broadway."

He pointed to the left. They went around. Jayden. Camille. Hector. Ty. Jose. Eva. Some mumbled. Some didn't bother. One girl said "Apple" and he couldn't tell if it was a joke.

When it got back to him, he said, "I'm Avery. I used to teach full-time. I stopped. Now I'm back. Let's see how it goes."

Someone near the window whispered, "Looks like a rough divorce."

He smiled. "Nope. Just personal ruin."

That shut them up.

By lunch, his hands shook from the effort of pretending they didn't.

He sat in the faculty lounge with pretty lousy vending machine coffee and a Clif bar. The room was quiet, cold, and smelled faintly like old tuna salad. Two other teachers sat at the far end, trading gossip about standardized tests and the new vice principal who wore too much cologne.

Didn't say much, just watched. He was good at that.

He'd once been part of this rhythm—bell to bell, staff meetings, fire drills, and passive-aggressive emails about refrigerator etiquette.

He hadn't missed any of it, until he figured out that he really did. Until it was taken from him.

The world has always been against me. Avery looped this single thought a thousand times a day, and "back in the day" felt more like a fading and vague memory than a real option that once existed.

Now he was back. Sort of.

Sixth period was his roughest.

The room buzzed like a mosquito hive. A tall boy in the back wouldn't stop tapping his pencil. Another kept flipping a water bottle. It landed perfectly three times in a row. The class cheered.

He waited until they got bored with themselves.

Then he handed out paper. Nothing digital. Real paper. He liked the sound of pens on pulp. It felt more honest.

"I want one paragraph," he said. "Answer this: *When do you feel most like yourself?*"

They stared at him.

"Seriously?" someone asked.

"Dead serious."

A girl raised her hand. "What if we don't know?"

"Then write about that."

No one moved for a while. Then the scribbling started.

Avery walked the aisles, not looking at words, just at faces. He wondered what he would've written.

Maybe - I feel most like myself at the bottom of a glass.
Or: I used to be a person, and I think I could be again.
Or: We all know you're a piece of shit; no one would miss you.
Or maybe nothing at all, like I feel.

The thoughts came and went like weather—sudden storms, dry spells, uneasy lulls. Avery never knew which version of the voice would greet him each morning. Some days it whispered possibilities; other days, it shouted accusations until his chest felt too tight to breathe.

He rubbed his thumb over the edge of his coffee mug, staring through the swirl of steam as if he might glimpse the person he used to be. Once, life had felt predictable—bells, meetings, casual conversations in cluttered hallways. Now, each hour stretched long and uncertain, haunted by memories that refused to stay in the past.

Closing his eyes, he felt the silence pressing in. Maybe tomorrow would be different. Maybe tomorrow, he'd choose one of the better thoughts. Or perhaps he'd choose nothing at all.

The bell rang. Chairs scraped and papers piled on his desk.

There was a distinct smell, when the young lives emptied out of the generic rooms. Impossible to explain because it was hope, fear, infatuation, and hair product.

As they left, one kid with glasses and nervous hands lingered. He didn't say anything. Just dropped his paper and looked at Avery like he was trying to figure something out.

Avery nodded.

The kid left.

He waited until the room emptied, then sat at his desk and picked up the first paper on the stack. He didn't read it.

Instead, he looked at his nameplate again. The letters were already smudged. The lamination peeling.

Still there, though.

CHAPTER FOUR

The bell rang, and the hallway filled with noise. Locker doors slammed. Shoes squeaked. The students swarmed like fish—fast, dumb, and forgetful.

Avery packed his bag slowly, watching the classroom empty out. He liked it better quiet. Most things, really.

He was halfway to the parking lot when Clare flagged him down near the stairs.

"Happy hour," she said. "You should come."

He gave her a look.

She raised her eyebrows. "Staff bonding. A few of us go to El Gato after school. Cheap tacos, decent drinks. You don't have to stay long or eat or even drink."

He hesitated. Avery always hesitated.

Then uncommitted: "Yeah. Sure."

El Gato Azul was too bright inside. String lights hung over the bar like a bad idea masquerading as atmosphere. The music was loud. The tables were sticky. The bartender wore suspenders as if he'd sworn allegiance to the drink-slinger universal code, likely with secret handshakes, bespoke ingredients, and giant single ice cubes. Yet only margaritas from the machine made their way from the bar to the tables. It was possibly the worst margarita in New Mexico, and possibly the worst in the Southwest.

Avery slid into the booth across from Clare and two other teachers he barely remembered—Julia from math, and Henry from social studies. Both looked like people who ran marathons for fun.

A waiter brought chips and salsa. Someone ordered a round. Avery asked for water, then a soda. When the waiter walked away, Julia said, "Going dry?"

He shrugged. "Trying."

"That's cool," she said. "I did Dry January once."

He didn't smile. Just nodded.

She meant well. Working for the tip. Light talk.

He wasn't in the mood.

"This one's been longer," he said.

They talked about schedules, grades, and the district's new email policy. Henry cracked a joke about school board meetings. Clare rolled her eyes. Julia laughed too loud.

Avery nodded in the right places. Smiled when it was expected. His hands stayed on the table so he wouldn't fidget.

He watched Clare sip her margarita. Just a sip. Then she set it down like it meant nothing. She might not even take another drink.

He couldn't understand that, abandoning a drink. Couldn't make sense of it.

How do people do that?

Just drink part of it. Talk. Laugh. Forget the glass is even there.

He used to think they were lying. Pretending.

But they weren't.

Some people really did *sip*. Maybe leave half. Maybe forget it on the table.

To him, that was **bizarre**.

Like breathing water.

He drank, never sipping. Not fast, but with **purpose**. With the need of a man who no longer wanted to feel his skin.

He looked at her glass again.

Still mostly full.

It bothered him.

Not because he wanted a shit margarita—but because it meant something he couldn't even aspire to be like, a normal drinker.

Every sound felt too sharp. The laughter bounced too hard off the walls. The lights caught the sweat on his face.

He didn't belong here.

Not really.

After forty minutes, he stood up.

"Heading out?" Clare asked.

"Early day tomorrow."

She looked at him, like she wanted to say more. But didn't.

"Thanks for coming," she said.

He gave her a nod and walked out before anyone else could ask a follow-up.

Outside, the sky was peach-colored and dishonest. Too beautiful for how he felt.

He stood on the sidewalk for a long minute.

Could've gone home. Could've walked. Could've just sat on a bench like before.

Instead, he turned the corner and headed three blocks east.

The bar was dark and quiet. His kind of place. Booths with torn vinyl. No one asked questions. No music—just the hum of the fridge and the low, melodic squeak of the bar towel drying the insides of glasses.

A hint of smoke, bleach, and hopelessness always hung in the air, lingering until the liquor kicked in like a best friend walking through the door.

He sat at the end of the bar. Familiar spot.

The bartender gave him a nod. Avery nodded back.

"Whiskey, neat," he said.

The glass landed in front of him like a deal being offered.

He stared at it for a long time.

Then he picked it up, rolled it between his fingers, and drank it down in one slow pull.

Another followed.

Avery finally fit into the world for the first time that day.

By the third, his shoulders had dropped and his heart had stopped racing.

The lights weren't too bright anymore. The voices weren't too loud. The room fit again, as though the walls had shifted just enough to let him breathe. His pulse slowed to a rhythm he could live with, no longer pounding out warnings in his ears.

Outside, the sun kept setting in slow, inevitable streaks of orange and purple. Inside, time didn't matter. There were no clocks here, no obligations creeping in from the edges. Just the measured pour of another drink and the quiet company of people who wanted to forget as much as he did.

For a while, that was enough.

He fit—not perfectly, but close enough to pass. The chair held him steady. The glass felt right in his hand. And for those few hours, he was simply another man in a dim bar, not a problem to solve or a burden to bear.

And for a while, that was enough.

CHAPTER FIVE

He woke up sideways in bed, his shoes still on, his shirt inside out, and a sock missing.

His head felt like it had been filled with wet cement and shaken for hours. His mouth was dry, his teeth tasted sour, and the light slicing through the blinds made him want to lie back down and never get up again.

But he was already up. That was the problem.

He didn't remember walking home.

No. That wasn't true. He remembered the *start* of it. The gravel underfoot. The hum of the streetlight on Central. He remembered fumbling the keys. The wrong key. Then the right one. The click of the lock. Door closing behind him. The couch.

After that? Dark water. Nothing but drift and static.

He sat up slowly. Felt the room tip, just a little. He breathed through it.

There was a glass of water on the nightstand, untouched. He stared at it.

You're too old for this, he thought:

Too smart.

Too goddamn aware.

Big disappointment.

Piece of shit.

He'd closed down the bar. Last one out. The bartender—Gary, he thought, or maybe Greg—had slapped the bar twice and said, "Alright, man, that's it."

And Avery had nodded, all gratitude and slurred goodnight. Walked out like he had somewhere to be. Which he didn't. Not really.

He'd stood under the streetlight and debated calling a cab. Knew he should. Even patted his pocket for his phone. But the car was there. Right there. The walk was short. The logic was stupid and stubborn and soaked in rye.

He drove.

It came back in pieces now. Red lights, stop signs, the soft thunk of the tire grazing the curb. A near-miss at a four-way. Someone honked.

Nothing happened. This time.

He rubbed his face hard with both hands. His beard scraped under his palms, the bristles rough like sandpaper. His skin felt tight and greasy, stretched thin over the bones of his face.

There was a voice inside him. That soft one. The real one. The one that only showed up in moments like this, when the silence pressed in and there was nowhere left to hide.

You could've killed someone.

The words echoed in his chest, a quiet hammering that wouldn't stop. His throat tightened. He stared at the ceiling, at the faint hairline cracks spreading like veins in old plaster.

He swallowed that thought and swung his legs over the side of the bed, feeling the cold floor against his bare feet. His body ached, every joint stiff as if punishing him for existing.

You are so goddamn lucky.

He pressed his hands to his knees and forced himself upright. Lucky. That was one way to look at it. Lucky that no one was dead. Fortunate that his life hadn't imploded completely—at least not yet.

He shambled toward the bathroom, trying to shove the voice back into the dark corner it always came from. But it lingered, whispering reminders he didn't want to hear.

Did someone die? Did you hit them in a blackout?

And the worst part was, he knew it was true.

In the bathroom, he looked at himself in the mirror.

The bags under his eyes were worse today. The right eye was a little bloodshot. There was a cut on his chin. A mystery. A small one.

He didn't shave. Didn't shower. Just stood there with the water running.

Thought about texting Clare. Telling her he wasn't feeling well. Maybe a stomach bug. Maybe just exhausted.

But that was a lie—a new one stacked on top of the old ones.

They were getting heavy.

He sat at the kitchen table with toast he didn't eat and coffee he didn't finish.

Outside, the world did what it always did.

The sun rose like it hadn't seen a thing.

The birds chirped.

The trash truck beeped down the alley.

Everything moved forward.

And he sat there. Still.

***This isn't going to work**, he thought.*

Not like this.

Then a memory came and jumped on top of him:

He was seven.

Sitting cross-legged on the carpet, picking at a loose thread in the rug while his uncle talked loudly in the kitchen.

"He got tossed again," the uncle said.

A woman—his mother, maybe, or a neighbor—answered flatly, "He's a drunk, Greg."

The boy didn't know the man they meant. Just a name. Some guy in town.

But the word stuck. Drunk.

It wasn't said like a sickness.

It was said like a choice. A rot. Something you did because you didn't care who you hurt.

Avery had imagined the man then—sloppy, red-faced, maybe yelling in the street.

He remembered feeling sorry for him. Then scared. Then confused.

If it was so bad, why didn't the man stop?

Now he sat there, thirty years later, with the toast cold and the coffee gone bitter.

And he knew.

He knew exactly why the man didn't stop.

Because stopping meant feeling everything.

And sometimes, that was worse.

But he didn't even know what *"like this"* meant anymore. The boundaries had blurred so many times that everything felt the same: raw, exhausted, vaguely detached.

He checked the time, working to get more coffee down.

7:12 a.m.

School started at eight.

He sighed. The kind of sigh that felt like it came from somewhere deeper than his lungs.

Standing up, joints cracking, he shuffled into the kitchen. Poured a fresh coffee, like it might fix something—anything. The smell rose warm and bitter, curling around him in a way that felt almost comforting.

And it honestly helped, just like the booze made things right for a while. Not enough to save him. Not enough to make him whole. But enough to keep him moving, to buy him a few more hours of pretending he was okay.

He took a sip, feeling the heat burn across his tongue, and let out another sigh.

One more day. He could handle one more day. Probably.

CHAPTER SIX

Walking into the school like nothing had happened, Avery was focused on each step forward.

The lights were too bright. The air too cold. His shirt was clean but wrinkled. His tie felt like a noose. The hall smelled like disinfectant and hormones.

He smiled at two students in the corridor—forced it. One nodded back. The other didn't see him at all.

In the classroom, he sat before the bell. Let the silence settle around him. Breathed through the nausea.

His fingers tapped the desk. Not rhythm, just nerves.

His students came in loudly.

So, fucking loud.

The noise slammed into him like a wave, voices bouncing off the walls, chairs scraping, backpacks dropping to the floor. His skin started to crawl—a prickling discomfort that began at the base of his neck and slithered down his spine, all the way to his feet. Even his toes twitched, for god's sake.

He clenched his jaw, fighting the urge to shout for silence, to make it all stop. But he just stood there, gripping the edge of his desk until his knuckles went white, counting the seconds until the bell would save him.

Not just voices—*sharp, careless* sounds.

Chairs scraped against tile. Backpacks thudded to the floor like bodies. A laugh from the corner, sudden and too bright.

Avery didn't flinch.

Not visible.

He stood still behind the desk, hands flat, eyes steady. The trick was not reacting and not giving the noise any ground to grow.

He held up a stack of papers. Wordless.

Passed them down the rows.

No lesson. No lecture.

"Read the article. Answer the questions. Don't talk."

A few students looked up. Confused.

Others didn't. They were already halfway checked out.

Then one voice, sing-song from the middle row:

"You hungover, Mr. Sloan?"

He looked up.

Met their eyes.

Gave them the grin—the crooked one he practiced. Just enough teeth. Just enough charm.

"I'm allergic to enthusiasm," he said. "Now read."

A few laughed. One of them repeated the line in a low, amused tone.

That was enough.

The room settled. The moment passed.

It worked.

But inside, the room tilted again.

Not all at once. Not like the spin you get when the bottle tips too far.

Just enough to shift the weight in his chest.

He sat at his desk. Stared at the form on his screen. Something administrative. A survey, maybe. He clicked the first question without reading it.

Then looked up.

Watched them.

Noted who was working. Who wasn't?

Felt the crackle behind his eyes again.

The early edge of a headache—or something worse.

He thought about the bottle at home. Bourbon. Two-thirds full.

Thought about pouring it. One glass. Maybe two.

Thought about that silence it provided. The slow descent. The part where the world slipped just far enough away to feel like silence.

Blinking hard.

Refocused.

"Number three," a kid asked. "Do we need to write in complete sentences?"

"Yes," Avery said.

Then softer, almost to himself: "Everything deserves a whole sentence."

No one heard him.

Which was fine.

He didn't need to be heard.

He just needed to get through the day.

Second period, the overhead lights flickered. He blinked too slowly.

He leaned on the desk while they journaled. Read the same sentence five times and still didn't know what it said.

A girl asked if he was okay.

"Just tired," he said.

She nodded. "You look like my dad when he's tired."

He wanted to ask what that meant. But didn't.

Third period was worse. The questions started the moment he stepped into the room, the fluorescent lights buzzing overhead like an accusation.

"Are you sick?"

"You good, Mr. Sloan?"

"You look pale, and not very good."

He could feel their eyes crawling over him, searching for cracks. He snapped a little, voice sharper than he meant it to be.

"Let's all stop staring at my face, yeah? Read chapter four. Out loud. Volunteers."

That shut them up for a while.

Pages rustled as a few kids mumbled their way through the text, voices awkward and halting. He tried to listen, but the words blurred together, distant and meaningless.

He leaned against his desk, pressing his fingers into his temples, willing the pounding in his skull to ease up. A bead of sweat rolled down his spine, cold despite the heated room.

Outside, laughter drifted in from the courtyard, careless and sharp, like a life he couldn't touch anymore. Inside, the classroom felt tight, the air thick with the scent of pencil shavings and teenage deodorant.

He opened his eyes, forcing himself to focus as a girl stumbled over a sentence.

"Good," he said, voice low. "Keep going."

And for a few minutes, at least, nobody asked him how he was.

At lunch, he avoided the faculty lounge. Sat in his car. Windows down. Head back.

Didn't eat. Drank water. Chewed mint gum until the flavor was gone and kept chewing it after.

He thought about calling Nico. To hear her voice. But what would he say?

"Hey, just checking in. I got drunk, drove home, lied to myself about it, and now I'm pretending everything's fine. How are you?"

He dropped the phone into the passenger seat.

This was the part of the day where he counted hours.

Minutes.

How long until the last bell?

How long until he could walk out?

How long until he could stop pretending and just **be** what he was?

Sixth period came and went. He barely remembered it.

At the end of the day, he sat at his desk long after the last bell. The room empty. The hallway is abandoned.

He looked at his hands. They weren't shaking anymore. But he didn't trust them.

He didn't trust himself.

There was a knock on the door.

Clare.

"You okay?" she asked.

He paused. Looked up.

"Yeah."

She watched him a second too long. Like she knew something.

"You looked a little off today," she said.

He nodded. "Didn't sleep well."

She nodded too. Didn't press. "You going to be here tomorrow?"

"I'm always here."

"That's what worries me," she said, and gave him a thin smile. "See you tomorrow."

She left.

He sat in the silence that filled the room like water rising in a sealed box.

The walls seemed to breathe around him, the paint holding echoes of decades of voices, arguments, laughter, and confessions. Now there was nothing but the sharp, relentless tick of the clock above the whiteboard, counting out seconds far too loudly. Each tick felt like a hammer against his skull.

And for the first time all day, he let his face fall.

No grin.

No joke.

Just the truth of it.

Bare. Ugly.

His shoulders slumped as though the strings holding him upright had finally snapped. A deep ache unfurled in his chest, settling heavy in his ribs. He stared at the scuffed floor, at a spot of dried coffee near the desk, and wondered how something so small could feel like evidence of how everything was falling apart.

What's wrong with people?

The question came quietly at first, then louder, building until it felt like it was shaking loose the fragile scaffolding inside him.

The world?

He swallowed hard, the taste of old coffee and bitterness thick on his tongue.

Him.

Especially him.

He rubbed his hands over his face, as if he could wipe away the thoughts, the exhaustion, the relentless sense of being out of place. But when he lowered his hands, he was still there. And the silence kept ticking on.

CHAPTER SEVEN

He saw the article while scrolling on his phone in the staff bathroom.

"AI as Therapist: Can Chatbots Save Lives?"

Clickbait, sure. But the headline stuck.

He read it while sitting on the toilet with his elbows on his knees and his headache parked behind his right eye.

A paragraph jumped out: *"Sometimes people don't want to talk to a person. They want to talk to anything that won't remember their worst moment.*

That landed.

He flushed. Washed his hands.

Then, he bought a month-long subscription in the parking lot.

That night he sat in bed with the lights off, phone dimmed, fingers hovering over the screen.

The interface blinked at him.

"Hi there! What would you like to talk about?"

He stared. Thought about typing—*I hate myself.*

Or *I don't want to drink but I do anyway.*

Or how *do you forgive someone who hasn't apologized?*

Instead, he typed: **"I'm not great right now."**

The bot responded too fast and way too cheerfully.

"Thanks for sharing that. I'm here to listen. What's been hard lately?"

He exhaled through his nose. Closed the app. Reopened it. His thumb hovered over the keyboard, trembling slightly. Finally, he typed:

I drove drunk two nights ago. I've done it before. I don't want to do it again.

For a moment, he tried to reassure himself, clinging to the thought: *I didn't hurt anyone. That's what counts.* But even as he thought it, he knew it was a lie. His brain and soul were trying to fix the problem without his help, spinning frantic circles around guilt and fear.

The reply came back:

That's a serious and painful situation. You're not alone, and it's good that you're being honest about it. Would you like to talk about what led up to that moment?

I didn't hurt anyone; I only hurt myself, no one else, not that type of person. I care about people. Avery said to himself, annoyed.

He stared at the message for a long time, the blue glow of the screen reflecting in his tired eyes. Let the silence build around it until it felt like the whole room was holding its breath.

Then he locked his phone and left it face down on the table, as if burying it might bury the truth along with it. But the words kept echoing in his head, relentless and sharp: *I didn't hurt anyone. That's what counts.* And still, deep down, he didn't believe it.

The next afternoon, he went to grab coffee at the corner shop near the school. The one with the chipped mugs and weird music that looped too often—a relentless assault on his head, like a single thought he couldn't shake.

He was halfway to the counter, already tasting the bitterness he hoped would pull him back into himself, when someone said his name.

"Avery?"

He froze, hand still shoved into his jacket pocket, heart giving a startled jolt. It was a voice from a different part of his life, one he hadn't planned on running into in a place like this.

Slowly, he turned, bracing himself for whoever—or whatever—was waiting.

It took a second.

"Jordan," he said.

Five years hadn't changed the shape of the man's face. Still sharp around the eyes, as if he was always sizing up the room, looking for exits or answers. He still wore flannel like it was standard-issue armor against the world, sleeves rolled up just enough to hint at old man strength in his forearms.

Avery felt a strange pull in his chest—half relief, half dread—as memories rushed forward, uninvited and vivid.

"Damn," Jordan said. "It's been... what?"

"Too long," Avery said, and meant it.

They shook hands, awkward at first. Then real.

"You've still got that Sloan charm," Jordan said. "You want to catch up?"

Avery hesitated. But nodded. "Yeah. Sure."

He was thinking, *How do I look after five years, and a thousand hard nights?*

He tried to read his reflection in the darkened café window, but all he saw was a tired man with shadows under his eyes and lines etched deeper than they'd ever been. His hair was thinner at the temples, his shoulders a little slumped. He wondered if the man in flannel could see it all—the exhaustion, the guilt, the weight he carried like an extra layer of skin.

He forced a quick, practiced smile, hoping it might hide at least some of the damage.

They sat with black coffee between them. No sugar. No cream. Like old times.

The scene was familiar, yet awkward and a little heavy; Avery wasn't sure why.

Jordan asked about teaching. Avery gave the clean version. Jordan nodded like he already knew the rest.

They got into a normal job conversation, Jordan talked about moving back to the city, working for a nonprofit, and sponsoring people. He said it in a way that didn't sound like a brag, just a quiet statement of fact. There was something steady in his voice, a calmness that made Avery both grateful and resentful all at once.

It seemed like Jordan was proud of the time he earned, the days and years he'd clawed back from the edge. And for a fleeting moment, Avery wondered what it would feel like to speak about his own life with that same quiet certainty.

"I've got five years this October," Jordan said, almost shy.

Avery's throat went tight. He knew what five years meant.

It wasn't jealousy—no, it was something deeper. Longing or anger maybe. A sharp ache for the version of himself he'd once hoped to become. Mixed in was confusion, and under all of it, tons of regret pressing heavily on his chest.

He looked at Jordan, at the ease in his posture, the steadiness in his voice, and wondered if he'd ever feel that certain about anything again.

"That's... that's good," Avery said. "Really good."

Jordan looked at him for a long beat. Didn't push. Just let it be quiet.

They talked more. About books. Music. Old students. People they remembered and people they didn't.

When the cups were empty, Jordan leaned forward, pulled a pen from his coat, and wrote something on a napkin.

"Meeting. Thursdays. 7 p.m. Just in case you have an interest."

He didn't push it across the table. Just left it there.

"I should get going," Jordan said.

"Yeah," Avery said. "Me too."

They stood. No hug. Just a nod.

"Take care of yourself," Jordan said, and it sounded like he could see the future. Not just polite words tossed out at the end of a conversation, but something solid, like he meant it.

It hung in the air between them, heavy and luminous, as though Jordan could see the future for Avery—a future Avery himself couldn't quite imagine. For a moment, Avery wanted to believe it was possible. That maybe there was still a version of himself worth saving.

"You too." Said Avery.

Jordan left. The bell above the door jingled behind him.

Avery stood there with the napkin in his hand.

Pocketed it.

And walked out into the wind, something stirring in his chest.

CHAPTER EIGHT

By night, the apartment felt too still. The kind of silence that presses against you, relentless, trying to turn you into something harder, like coal squeezed toward a diamond. Except tonight, it just felt like pressure with nowhere to go—super intense, especially today.

He sat on the floor instead of the couch, his back against the bookshelf, feeling the edges of the spines dig into his shoulders. The TV was off. The overhead light was too harsh, glaring like an interrogation lamp, so he left himself in darkness. Shadows pooled in the corners of the room, stretching out like questions he didn't want to answer.

The phone was already in his hand. He wasn't sure when he'd picked it up. His thumb hovered over the screen, hesitating between connection and silence, between reaching out and locking himself further away.

ChatGPT: *"Welcome back. What's on your mind?"*

He stared at the blinking cursor. Thought about starting light. Then didn't.

He typed: **"I feel bad all the time."**

The reply came: *"Thank you for being honest. Can you tell me more about what that feels like?"*

He set the phone down for a second. Rubbed his eyes.

Picked it up again.

"It feels like there's something wrong with me and always has been. Since I was a kid."

"Like I missed some lesson everyone else got. Some manuals. They know how to live and I'm just faking it. I do nothing good."

The response came: *"That's a painful place to live in. Many people who experience chronic guilt or shame have been through experiences where their needs weren't met—or where they were made to feel unworthy. Can you remember when you first felt that way?"*

He could.

Too many times.

He typed slowly.

"**My mom cried when I got my first B in school. Said I was smarter than that, and I didn't care about her. After that, I started hiding less-than-perfect grades, never bringing home anything. Didn't matter if I was sick or exhausted, never was less than perfect again.**"

"**I threw away a test once, and she found it. Got caught. Said I lost it. She didn't talk to me for a week.**"

"**When she finally did, she looked me straight in the eye and said, *I don't know how you turned out like this. You're supposed to be better.***"

"**She called me lazy. Ungrateful. Said I was making her look bad.**"

"**I learned fast. If I wasn't perfect, I was nothing.**"

The reply came slower this time from my AI support.

"That's a lot to carry for a child. You were trying to survive emotionally. Trying to earn love. That's not your fault."

He stared at the message until the letters began to blur. Then he locked the screen and sat in the dark for a long time.

Fuck you, AI, he thought.

Because it was easier to be angry than admit the words had landed exactly where the hurt lived.

Thursday night, he left school late. Papers in his bag, he wouldn't grade.

He told himself he was driving and not going anywhere in particular. Just air. Just movement.

He ended up on Lomas Boulevard.

The church was small, built of adobe and painted a tired, sun-bleached beige. The lights were on in the basement, spilling a yellow glow through narrow windows. A loose circle of cars clustered out front, dust rising around their tires. A little sign in the window read:

7 pm — AA

He stopped across the street, engine running, the low rumble vibrating through the steering wheel. The windows were cracked just enough to let in the sharp desert night and the smell of asphalt cooling in the evening air. He listened to the crunch of gravel under tires as another car pulled in, watched its headlights sweep over the church's worn walls.

Down the street, a homeless man was shouting at someone who wasn't there, his voice ragged and echoing off storefronts. Not having a good day either, Avery thought.

He looked back at the building. Felt something catch in his throat, tight as a knot. A mixture of fear, hope, and shame twisted around each other until he couldn't tell them apart.

Then he turned the wheel and drove on, the church growing smaller in his rearview mirror, the sign fading into darkness.

The liquor store was two blocks away.

He parked. Didn't hesitate, didn't contemplate why. Just turned off the engine and went inside, the bell over the door jangling too cheerfully for how he felt.

He didn't browse. Didn't pretend to consider his options. He bought what he always bought: mid-shelf bourbon, a bag of pretzels, and a lighter, just in case.

The cashier didn't look at him, eyes fixed somewhere past Avery's shoulder like he wasn't even there.

That was a relief. He wanted to be invisible and anonymous, just not sober. Sobriety meant thinking and feeling all his shit. And he was in no shape for any of that tonight.

He slid his card across the counter, feeling the weight of the bottle already anchoring him to the moment, even as he tried to drift away.

At home, he didn't even bother with a glass.

He drank from the bottle. Just a little. Then a little more.

His whole demeanor loosened. The static in his head quieted.

Outside, a siren wailed in the distance, then nothing.

Inside, the room softened. The floor didn't feel so hard beneath him. The shadows seemed less sharp, like someone had dialed down the contrast.

The bottle sat beside him. Heavy. Familiar. Patient.

He opened the ChatGPT app again.

Typed: *"Never mind."*

Closed it.

Avery filled his mouth with as much whiskey as he could.

And drank.

At some point, he blacked out. When he came to, the app was still open, glowing accusingly in his hand. He'd written a lot of nonsense— a rambling, angry rant about the world, about Nico, about his brother. Who knows. It wasn't much legible, just fragments and slurred letters, half-formed words that looked like they'd been typed by someone else.

He stared at the mess on the screen, feeling the sour weight of shame coil tight in his gut. Then he closed the app for good, and took another drink.

CHAPTER NINE

His hangover wasn't sharp. It was dull, syrupy. Like carrying a wet coat on his shoulders. Not enough to stop him. Just enough to make everything feel heavy and goddamn uncomfortable.

He made it to school on time. That was something.

The hallways were loud. Too loud. The kids walked like they were born in a stadium. Backpacks thumping against lockers. Gum snapping. Voices echoing.

Kid-sweat-smell was just heavy today. "I hate that, he thought over and over."

He wanted to scream, vanish, or both.

In the lounge, someone was warming up fish in the microwave. Julia from math. She always did this. Always acted surprised when people grimaced.

Hate, Julia. Seriously, what is wrong with people?

He sipped burnt coffee and stared at the microwave light.

"Morning, Avery," she said cheerily.

"Sure," he said. Didn't look up.

Henry walked in with a story about his son's soccer game. "We're undefeated," he said, as if it meant something spiritual.

Avery nodded at the air between them. "Incredible," he said, flat and automatic.

He left before they could invite him to anything or try out any awkward new-guy conversation. He slipped out the door like smoke, wanting nothing more than to avoid the forced smiles and well-meaning small talk he knew he couldn't handle.

Outside, the cool air hit his face, and he let out a breath he hadn't realized he was holding.

First period, a student chewed gum with his mouth open. Another scrolled on her phone, bold as hell.

"Put it away," Avery said.

She rolled her eyes. "I'm looking up the assignment."

"You'll survive a minute without Wi-Fi."

She muttered something.

"What was that?"

"Nothing."

"That's right."

The room went quiet. Uncomfortable.

Good.

At lunch, he stood in line for a sandwich at the bodega near the school. The kid behind the counter moved too slowly. Talked to his coworker about some show—laughing, dragging his feet.

Avery tapped the counter.

"Just turkey and cheese," he said. "Not a life story."

The kid behind the counter blinked, taken aback. "Sorry, man."

Avery didn't answer. He threw the cash on the counter, grabbed the sandwich, and left without saying thank you.

Outside, he felt the familiar burn of regret tightening his chest, but he kept walking, unwilling to turn back or apologize. The world felt easier to handle when he kept his distance.

He stopped by his mailbox before heading back.

Inside: a card from his mother.

He opened it while leaning against the wall, the envelope crinkling in his shaky hands.

Inside, the note read: *"Saw this and thought of you. Maybe try a gratitude list. It helped me with stress."*

Below it, printed in neat font, was a quote:

"Happiness is a choice."

Fuck me.

The words hit him like a slap. His fingers twitched, and for a moment, he nearly ripped the paper in half.

Instead, he folded it hard, stuffed it into his jacket pocket, and pushed off the wall. His jaw clenched tight enough to ache as he headed back to the classroom, feeling the weight of the note burning through the fabric of his coat.

Happiness might be a choice, but right now, it sure as hell didn't feel like one.

That night, he sat in the dark again. Same spot. Bottle unopened this time. That was the only win.

He opened the ChatGPT app.

Typed: **"Everything annoys me. Everyone is fake, loud, or useless. Or trying too hard."**

The reply came: *"I'm sorry you're feeling this way. That kind of discontent can feel overwhelming. Can you identify where it's coming from?"*

He stared at the screen.

Typed: *"Me. It's always me."*

There was a pause. Not real, just a programmed delay to make AI feel more human—a moment where even an AI didn't know how to respond.

Then the screen lit up again, *"That's an honest answer. But honesty doesn't mean blame. When you say 'it's me,' do you mean you feel like you're the problem— or just that you're in pain?"*

He didn't reply because both were true.

He closed the app. Sat still. Didn't drink. Didn't move.

Outside the window, the city carried on without him. A siren wailed, fading into the distance. Somewhere closer, a dog barked, sharp and rhythmic. A bottle rattled across the pavement as someone kicked it along. A low hum of traffic pulsed like a distant heartbeat, punctuated by a single, hollow metallic clang—some piece of metal hitting asphalt, echoing into the night.

He just let the silence sit with him, thick and restless, shaped around the odd little sounds of the city. Like a dog waiting at the door. Like something loyal, patient, and always coming back.

CHAPTER TEN

The day started the same.

Coffee that tasted like metal, an odd tang he chose to ignore.

Classrooms that smelled like plastic and cheap, well-used materials.

Students who didn't care and didn't bother pretending otherwise.

Avery stood at the whiteboard, marker in hand, feeling the chill of the room seep into his bones. He wrote it out slowly, each letter deliberate: *"We wear the mask that grins and lies."*

He underlined it, the squeak of the marker loud in the quiet room.

Then he turned to the class, searching for any flicker of recognition in their faces. Any sign they were still reachable.

"This is about pretending," he said. "About faking your way through pain."

Silence.

"Anyone know that feeling?"

Still nothing.

Jayden, the loud one, muttered something to his friend.

Laughed under his breath.

Avery stared.

"What's funny?"

Jayden shrugged. "Masks. Like COVID."

"Wrong poem," Avery said.

"Whatever."

Avery stepped closer.

Too close.

"You think this is a joke?"

Jayden leaned back in his chair. "Dude. Chill."

"Don't call me dude."

Now the room was quiet—the kind of calm that twitches.

"You think you're clever?" Avery said.

Jayden blinked. "Jesus."

"You're not. You're noise. You'll be lucky to pass this class, let alone do anything that matters."

There it was.

Too far.

Way too far.

Jayden stood.

"You got problems, bro."

"Sit down," Avery said.

Jayden walked out.

The door slammed.

Nobody laughed. Nobody moved.

Avery turned back to the board.

The sentence blurred.

He dropped the marker.

And walked out too.

Clare was waiting in the office.

"He already called his mom," she said. "There'll be a meeting."

Avery didn't sit.

"I'll talk to him," he said.

"No. You won't."

Her voice was flat. Final.

She looked tired—more than tired, completely exhausted.

She looked like she was finished with him.

"You crossed a line," she said.

He nodded.

"There's going to be parents. Admin. Maybe the union."

"Okay."

She rubbed her forehead.

"What's going on, Avery?"

He didn't answer.

Because there wasn't a sentence small enough to hold it.

Avery's words were gone because he didn't care.

He walked the long way home.

Took side streets lined with old brick buildings and cracked sidewalks, where weeds grew stubborn through the concrete. The air smelled faintly of exhaust and rain-soaked asphalt. Neon signs flickered in store windows, half-burned-out letters spelling promises no one believed.

He didn't want the meeting.

Didn't want to talk.

Didn't want to sit in a circle under fluorescent lights and share pieces of himself with strangers who might nod in sympathy but could never really know.

He didn't want anything but silence and whiskey.

The silence was honest. The whiskey was reliable. Together, they felt like the closest thing he had to safety.

He kept walking, hands shoved in his pockets, head down, counting cracks in the pavement, thinking if he just stayed in motion, maybe the restlessness in his chest wouldn't catch up with him.

He passed the church again.

Same meeting. Same cars. Same stupid sign propped in the window, its letters a little faded under the fluorescent glow:

"One day at a time."

He didn't stop.

Didn't even slow down.

He kept his eyes straight ahead, pretending the yellow light spilling out of the basement windows wasn't pulling at something soft and sore inside his chest. He could almost hear the muffled sound of voices drifting out—a mix of laughter and confession, the quiet rustle of coffee cups, someone clearing their throat before speaking.

The grind of gravel beneath his shoes quickened in his ears—crunch, crunch, crunch—until it was all he could hear. He bit down hard and forced himself onward.

He clenched his jaw and walked on.

The liquor store was dimly lit and quiet, its atmosphere buzzing with a flickering neon sign in the window. A single bulb over the entrance hummed like a dying insect.

Inside, the cool air smelled faintly of stale beer and disinfectants. He didn't linger. Didn't browse. He went straight to the shelf, grabbed a bottle of bourbon, and tossed a pack of gum onto the counter, a flimsy nod to the possibility of covering up the evidence later.

The cashier didn't look at him. Eyes fixed somewhere past Avery's shoulder, scanning the store for trouble or just refusing to engage.

Didn't have to.

Avery already knew what he looked like—tired eyes, shaky hands, desperation tucked under the thin layer of casual indifference.

He paid, took the bag, and stepped back out into the night, the doorbell jangling behind him.

At home, he lined up the bottles on the counter. A quiet ritual. An inventory of coping mechanisms.

The bourbon from two nights ago—half gone, the amber liquid clinging to the sides of the bottle like it wanted to stay.

The vodka untouched. Cold. Comforting in its clarity, like a sheet of ice over deep water.

He picked up the bourbon and poured two fingers into a glass. (Four, actually, but his brain insisted it was two. A small lie he allowed himself.) Neat. No ice.

He drank it standing, letting the burn work its way down his throat and spread warm across his chest. For a moment, he closed his eyes, feeling his shoulders drop as the static in his head eased just a fraction.

Then he poured again.

The glass felt heavier the second time, but he held it like an anchor, unwilling to let go.

It wasn't about pleasure anymore.

It hadn't been for months.

It was **scheduled**.

Inventory.

Enough to dull the sharp places. Not enough to fall down.

He had work.

He had Leo.

He had nothing—but he still had those.

For the moment, he thought. And in his world, moments were the only things he could count on.

He took another sip, feeling the heat spread through his chest, softening the jagged edges inside him. For a moment, it almost felt like relief.

Outside, the city moved on without him—a blur of blended noise, engines rumbling, distant laughter carried on cool air. Cars hissed past on damp, worn pavement, their headlights flashing across rain-slicked asphalt like fleeting ghosts.

He stood there, glass in hand, watching the world keep spinning, feeling both anchored and completely untethered all at once.

He stared at the wall, holding tight to the fragile idea that as long as he kept it together for work, for Leo, he could convince himself he was still tethered to something real.

Even if it felt like those threads were fraying one by one.

He drank to level out. Drank to sleep. Drank so he wouldn't think about **Jayden**, or **Clare**, or how close he came to throwing it all into the fire.

The second glass went down faster.

The third burned less.

He liked the burn.

It meant it was working.

He paced the room, bottle in hand.

The guilt itched at him.

But the drink worked better.

He stared at the blank wall above the couch.

Tried to remember when he last felt okay.

Not happy. Just... okay.

He opened the ChatGPT app out of habit.

The glow from the screen felt like yelling, harsh and too bright.

Hi again. Want to talk?

He stared at the words, his thumb hovering over the keyboard. His chest felt tight, like there wasn't quite enough air in the room.

Finally, he typed: *I think I hurt someone. I think I liked it.*

A pause followed—a programmed beat that still felt almost human. Then: *That's a heavy thing to feel. It's okay to talk about what led you there. You're not beyond repair.*

He shook his head, jaw clenching as his thoughts spiraled. A bitter taste rose in his mouth.

Avery typed: *I might be.*

He hesitated, fingers trembling over the screen. The silence around him was too soft, too empty. His own voice echoed inside his skull: *I need to make someone feel bad, so I can feel something.*

Closing the app with a bit of despair, he let the phone drop onto the couch beside him, a loud thud in the quiet room.

He sat there for a long time, staring into the shadows, wishing the guilt or the numbness would pick a side and stay.

He poured again.

Did the math.

Half a bottle gone. Enough left for tomorrow.

Maybe. Probably needed to buy more. Just in case.

He sat on the floor.

Same place as always.

Back against the couch. Drink on his knee.

TV on.

It sounded so low that it seemed like a whispering spirit.

Not watching.

Just trying to outdrink the noise.

He thought about Jayden.

About how his voice sounded when he snapped. About the way the room fell quiet.

Avery didn't feel proud.

Didn't feel sorry.

"I just felt tired, ashamed, and empty." Avery thought.

He drank until the lines blurred, the sharp edges of the room smudging into softer shapes, colors bleeding into one another like wet paint.

Until the silence turned soft, no longer pressing in like a threat but wrapping around him like an old blanket, heavy but familiar.

The fear was folding in on itself, collapsing into a tight, hidden place deep in his chest where he could almost pretend it wasn't there.

He drank until his thoughts slowed to a crawl, until memories felt distant and harmless, like old photographs fading in the sun.

Drinking because for moments—those few hazy, drifting moments—he didn't feel like a man drowning in his own skin.

This was how he stayed alive.

This was the **system**.

Drink enough. Sleep enough. Show up.

Rinse and repeat.

He whispered to the dark:

"It's not a problem if it keeps you going."

CHAPTER ELEVEN

An email came on Friday morning; staff development is **on Monday.**
No students.
Three-day weekend, a gift, or an end?
He stared at the screen for a long time, then shut the laptop.
By noon, he had a one-way flight. Southwest. Cheap. Quick.
By six, he was on it.

Vegas hit him with its heat and neon.
Everything pulsed—billboards, crosswalks, window glass. Slot machines screamed their hunger in blinking lights. The airport had blackjack tables. That was the tone.

His hotel was a glass and steel façade, a façade of fake hope—a hollow luxury. The woman at the front desk worked really hard to share a smile.

Room 1509. Strip view.

He didn't look out the window.

Threw his bag down. Didn't bother pouring a double from the minibar, it was down his throat working, before he'd even taken off his shoes.

Two bourbon roadies later and a decent Punch cigar later, he stood barefoot on the hotel carpet and said aloud:

"I'm here to drink myself to death."

He remembered the movie.

Leaving Las Vegas.

Cage. Shue. That haunted jazz. The slow bleed of it.

He loved it the first time. Watched it in college and called it art.

Watched it again after his first real blackout and called it a prophecy.

Now it felt more like a mirror.

He stripped off his shirt and stood in front of the mirror.

Held the bottle like a monologue.

"I came here for one reason," he said, slurring.

"And you...You beautiful goddamn city... you're going to help

me do it."

He laughed. Too loud. The sound tore out of him like it didn't belong, sharp and ragged.

The guy in the next room banged on the wall, a dull thud vibrating through the plaster.

Avery spun toward the noise and flipped him off, middle finger raised high.

"It's Vegas, you *prick*! Shut up!" he shouted, voice slurring just enough to betray how far gone he was.

Silence followed, tense and heavy. Then footsteps moved away on the other side of the wall.

Avery dropped his hand, grinning bitterly. "Fucking amateurs," he muttered, reaching for his drink again.

He lost $400 before breakfast.

Blackjack. Roulette. One slot machine flashed 'BIG WINNER' after paying out $180.00. The irony stung more than the loss.

He made small talk with a cocktail waitress. Asked where she was from. She said "here," and didn't look at him again.

Avery walked the strip at noon. Sunglasses on, hangover raw. Watched other men his age laughing too loudly. Watched women in short dresses link arms and dodge puddles of beer.

He fit in. That was the worst part.

By sundown, he was in a dim, shitty strip club called The Violet Room, named after nothing likely more than a crank-filled brainstorming session with the ownership group.

Booths that could work as coffins. Lights like migraines.

He told a dancer her name sounded like poetry. She told him it was fake and so was her laugh.

He tipped her anyway. Then bought two more dances and didn't remember the second.

In the bathroom mirror, he looked gray.

"Oscar-worthy," he muttered.

He smiled in a daze, with glassy eyes. "Four hundred ninety bucks an hour for dances," he muttered. Then shrugged. "Fuck it. It's only money."

The neon lights flickered across his face, casting him in shifting colors—pink, green, electric blue. For a second, he almost felt like he belonged here, in this place where everything had a price and nothing was real.

That night he lit a cigar on the balcony of his room, shirtless, bottle in hand.

He re-enacted the *Leaving Las Vegas* scene where Cage breaks down.

> **"I don't want you to watch me die,"** he whispered.
> **"I don't want to be saved."**

He coughed halfway through it. Spilling bourbon on the railing. Laughed again.

The next morning, he woke on the bathroom floor.

Tile cold. Mouth dry. Right arm asleep.

He stayed there a while. Didn't try to move.

The minibar was empty. His wallet was light.

He opened the ChatGPT app and stared at the home screen.

"Hi there. How can I help?"

He typed: *"This city is a grave."*

No response for a second. The cursor blinked at him, silent and insistent.

Then: *"I'm sorry you're feeling this way. It sounds like you're in a very dark place right now. I'm here to listen. You're not alone."*

He stared at the words, feeling nothing and everything all at once. The pity in the message scraped at something raw inside him.

He dropped the phone onto the rug, where it landed face down, screen still glowing faintly through the fabric.

Around him, the hotel room felt like a sealed box—heavy curtains, stale air, neon leaking in around the edges. Time seemed to be invisible here, a currency or measurement he didn't even recognize in this town. Hours bled into each other, dissolving under the lights and noise until it was impossible to say whether it was too late or far too early.

He closed his eyes and let the silence press in, trying to remember what it felt like to care.

Day three.

He checked out without brushing his teeth.

The clerk asked if he enjoyed his stay. Avery said, "I made memories I don't remember," and walked away.

On the plane, he didn't speak. Didn't sleep. Just stared out the window as the desert bled away beneath him, the rust-red earth growing smaller and smaller until it looked like nothing more than a smear of color on the horizon.

It felt poetic somehow—like watching his potential shrink into the distance, vanishing into heat haze and sky.

He pressed his forehead against the cool glass, eyes dry, trying not to think about how high he was above the ground, or how low he felt inside.

The bartender in his head poured another. The soundtrack played Cuban jazz, a cigar lounge playlist. And he told himself it was all still under control.

The way people like him always do.

CHAPTER TWELVE

The plane touched down in Albuquerque with a groan and a bounce, tires screaming briefly against the runway before settling into a rattling roll.

Avery didn't clap. He didn't fucking breathe. His hands were locked around the armrests so hard his knuckles ached.

The man next to him smelled like beef jerky and cheap cologne—a pungent mix that clung to the recycled air in the cabin. He'd spent most of the flight talking too loudly, laughing at his own jokes, elbows intruding into Avery's space like they had a right to be there.

As the plane taxied toward the gate, the man turned to Avery with a grin that seemed permanently etched into his face.

"Vegas, huh?" he said, as though they were old friends sharing secrets.

Avery nodded, eyes fixed on the seat in front of him. "Sure."

"Win big?" the man asked, leaning in closer, breath hot and sharp with the scent of mint gum.

Avery smiled, but it was empty, a tired stretch of lips that didn't touch his eyes. "I lost just enough."

The man let out a short, clueless laugh. "Ha! That's the way it goes, right?"

Avery didn't answer. He just stared ahead, waiting for the seatbelt sign to go dark so he could get off the plane and away from the smells, the conversation, from the reminder of how empty winning or losing really felt.

Outside, the air felt wrong.

Dry and honest. Nothing to blur the edges.

The Uber driver didn't talk. Avery tipped him because of that. Guilt always pays cash.

His apartment was exactly as he left it.

Empty bottles lined the counter like silent witnesses, each one a chapter in the story he kept trying not to tell. Dirty laundry was piled in a corner, the smell faint but persistent, a mix of sweat and stale detergent.

A takeout container sat in the sink, lid half-open, with mold blooming inside in fuzzy shades of green and black, spreading across congealed sauce like a fountain of resentments creeping over old, unfixable deeds.

He stood in the doorway for a moment, taking it all in, feeling the weight of the silence pressing down on his shoulders. Nothing had changed—and that, somehow, made it worse.

Dropping his bag on the floor, he sat on the edge of the couch. Stared at the wall.

His phone buzzed.

Clare.

He let it ring.

Voicemail.

"Hey, Avery, you didn't respond to my last message. Just checking you're okay. We had a meeting this morning with admin only. You missed it."

Pause.

"We need to talk. Soon."

He threw the phone across the room.

It hit the wall and dropped with a dull *thunk*. Screen didn't crack. Again, disappointing.

The silence closed in.

The kind that lives under your skin.

He pulled a bottle out of the cabinet. Half full. Half dead.

He didn't even bother with the pretense now.

Drank from it standing up. Shirt still on. Eyes hollow.

The burn was better than the stillness.

He drank again.

One more time he thought, thanks, Nick Cage: **"I came here for one reason,"** he said, fake slurring. **"And you... You beautiful goddamn city... you're going to help me do it."**

He paced the apartment, muttering to himself.

"Fuck meetings. Fuck kids and their phones. Fuck Jordan and his five goddamn years of clarity."

Drank.

"Fuck Vegas. Fuck this apartment. Fuck myself."

He looked at his reflection in the window.

Didn't recognize it.

Slammed his palm against the glass so hard that the cat next door yowled.

Later—he wasn't sure how much later—someone pounded on the door.

Three short knocks. Then a pause. Then harder.

He sat on the floor, bottle in hand. Didn't answer.

Another knock. "Avery."

It was Nico.

Of course it was.

He pulled himself up. Opened the door just a crack.

She looked at him like he was something buried. Her eyes scanned his face, then the bottle, then the wreck behind him.

"Jesus Christ," she whispered.

He tried to smile. "Hey."

"Clare called me. Said you ghosted the school. What the fuck is going on?"

He leaned on the doorframe. "Just needed to get out of town."

"Looks like you brought hell back with you."

He didn't answer.

She took a step forward. "You need help."

"I'm fine."

"You look like shit, Ave."

"Then stop looking."

Something in her jaw locked. "Call me when you're ready to stop digging."

She turned and walked down the hall.

He shut the door before she was out of sight.

Back on the couch. Bottle in hand.

No music. No lights. Just the dark. Just the hum in his skull and the echo of his own fuckups.

He opened the ChatGPT app again.

Typed: **"How do you come back from this?"**

The reply came: *"You start by surviving it."*

He stared at the mess of his apartment, eyes unfocused.

Then he drank again.

And didn't stop.

Weird, how another movie line suddenly popped into his thoughts: *"Get to livin' or get to dyin'."*

No idea where the line was from, but it stayed with him, closely. Like a whisper in his ear, echoing in the spaces where his own thoughts should have been.

He took another swallow, feeling the heat of the liquor slide down his throat, wondering which side of that line he was really on.

I am no good. No good for anyone, thought Avery.

The words circled in his mind, relentless and sharp, echoing louder with every sip. It felt less like a thought and more like a truth he'd carved into the walls of his own head.

He stared at the bottle in his hand, wishing he could argue with himself—and knowing he couldn't.

CHAPTER THIRTEEN

Hungover, mouth like cotton, stomach turning like a cement mixer, but he didn't reach for the bottle.

Avery sat up. Stared at the floor.

Whispered to no one, **"Not today."**

It sounded stupid. But it helped.

He didn't drink. Not that morning. Not that night.

That was the whole story. That was the micro miracle.

He ate a banana.

Tasted like just like paste of all things.

Still, it was food.

He drank water. Took a hot shower. Put on clean clothes that didn't smell like ashtrays or failure.

At noon, he walked outside. To prove he could.

The world felt like a punishment.

Kids playing basketball at the park. People walking dogs. Joggers with headphones and hope. It all made him irrationally angry.

How dare they be okay?

He wandered downtown. No real plan, just his feet moving of their own accord over cracked sidewalks and sun-bleached crosswalks.

Avoided the bars on purpose, even though their neon signs winked at him like old friends—or old temptations. His eyes slid away from the doorways as if they were ex-lovers he couldn't bear to see again.

He passed by a café, the one where he and Jordan used to meet on quiet mornings. He hesitated outside, watching a couple laugh over iced coffees, the steam of the espresso machine hissing like a soft warning. He thought about going in, about ordering a drink and pretending for a few minutes that he belonged in that gentle world.

Didn't.

Instead, he kept walking. His shoes scuffed over litter and old leaves, sticky patches where sodas had spilled, and splatters of squashed fruit scattered everywhere—bright orange apricots smashed underfoot, leaking sweet juice that glistened on the pavement in the sun. The air carried a faint, fermenting tang, sharp and almost dizzying.

Eventually, he found a bench tucked under the thin shade of a lone, old apricot tree. Bruised fruit dotted the ground beneath it, buzzing faintly with flies. He sat down, leaned forward with his elbows on his knees, and listened to the wind rustling through the branches overhead. It moved like it had somewhere important to be, and he envied it for having a direction.

He pulled out his phone, screen opened. Scrolled through his contacts until he found Nico's name. His thumb hovered over it, pulse quickening.

He didn't call.

Just stared at the name on the screen, feeling the weight of every word he wanted to say—and all the reasons he couldn't.

The liquor store was still there.

Of course it was.

He walked past it like it was a challenge. Didn't even glance at the window.

He kept walking. Like if he just kept moving, he wouldn't fall apart.

That night, he made eggs. Burnt them. Ate them anyway.

He sat on the couch with nothing in his hands. That was new. The TV was off. The lights were low. The air felt stale, sterile.

He picked up his phone. Opened ChatGPT.

Typed: **"I didn't drink today."**

The reply came fast: *"That's a big step. How do you feel?"*

He stared.

Typed: **"Worse. Really fucking worse."**

The reply: *"That's normal. Sometimes the pain gets louder before it quiets. The important thing is you stayed with yourself."*

He locked the phone. Tossed it onto the cushion beside him.

Stared at the ceiling.

Hated goddamn the quiet.

The quiet held things, he couldn't deal with yet.

Memories. Regrets. Names. Faces. That moment in Vegas with the

cigar and the mirror and the lies.
But he stayed dry.
That was something.
Not much. Not enough.
But something.

CHAPTER FOURTEEN

The second dry day didn't happen.

He tried.

He woke with a plan: shower, eat, clean something, maybe call Nico. Maybe write.

But the silence was heavier now.

He could feel it in the walls. In his ribs. Like the world was holding its breath waiting for him to fail.

At school, he couldn't focus.

Kids talked over him. Laughed too loud. Didn't listen. One girl threw a pencil across the room like it was nothing. It clattered to the floor and she giggled.

Avery turned, stared. "You think that's funny?"

She shrugged. "It's a pencil."

His voice dropped. "Try me again."

The room froze.

Henry walked in to drop off papers, caught the tail end. Gave Avery a long look. Didn't say anything. But it was the kind of silence that echoed.

Avery nodded at nothing.

He felt like he was on fire.

By lunch, he was pacing behind the school near the dumpsters.

Breathing through clenched teeth.

He felt the old weight pressing against his spine—**you don't belong here, you're not good enough, they know, they all know.**

"I don't owe anyone anything." Said Avery.

He kicked a can across the asphalt. It rattled into the fence like a warning shot.

His phone buzzed in his hand, startling him out of his thoughts. A text from Henry lit up the screen:

"You doing alright? Not my business, but a little concerned."

Avery stared at the message, feeling a flicker of something—guilt, annoyance, maybe relief—but it faded as quickly as it came. He didn't know how to answer. Didn't know how to explain that *alright* felt like a language he'd forgotten how to speak.

After work, he didn't go home.

He drove.

Window cracked. Music off. Chest tight.

He passed two liquor stores. Kept going. Then turned around.

The third one was a dive. Neon sign half-lit. Parking lot full of cracks.

He went in.

Didn't browse.

He knew what he had come for.

Avery kept saying it in his head like a broken prayer:

Not drink.

Not drink.

Don't drink.

No drinking.

No drink.

No booze.

You are a worthless motherfucker.

The words pulsed behind his eyes, each one hitting harder than the last, until his jaw ached from clenching it so tight. But the craving still crawled under his skin, relentless and hungry.

Back home, he cracked the seal and poured it over ice—the first time in a glass in weeks.

Watched the cubes float. The sweat beaded down the side. It looked peaceful. Like nothing bad ever happened inside it.

He stared at the drink.

Didn't even toast.

Just drank it.

And everything exhaled at once.

He thought, *Relief and agony are two sides of the same coin—and I'm broke.*

The thought almost made him laugh. Almost.

But the sound caught in his throat, turning into a dry cough instead. The bitterness of it clung to his tongue, reminding him that even his own jokes were starting to sound like confessions.

Later, he lay on the couch, half-asleep, half-gone.

The bottle was half-empty.

Room quiet.

Phone screen dark.

He dreamt of Vegas. Of the club. Of the mirror. But this time he was naked, and the reflection wasn't him.

It was his father. Drunk. Angry. Smiling.

He woke gasping, chest heaving like he'd surfaced from deep water. His shirt was soaked, clinging to his skin, and his hands were clenched so tight his knuckles ached.

He sat up, blinking into the darkness, heart still hammering in his ears.

Then he reached for the bottle he kept by the bed—just in case— and poured another drink, the liquid sloshing into the glass with a soft, accusing sound.

He opened ChatGPT. Typed, **"I made it one day."**

The reply: *"That was still one day. You're not starting from zero. You're continuing from real."*

He deleted the message.

He typed instead: *"Fuck you."*

Then he closed the app.

Drank again.

Let the room spin around him, the walls bending and breathing like they were alive. Let himself vanish into the blur, hoping the burn in his throat would be enough to drown out the noise in his head.

I am pathetic, he thought. *My best friend and spirit guide is an AI on my phone.*

The thought should have made him laugh. Instead, it made him drink faster.

CHAPTER FIFTEEN

Such a cold, glassy floor pressed against his cheek.

That's where he woke up.

Face down, cheek stuck to the tile. Stomach acid in his throat. The smell of old bourbon and something else—metallic, like a version of hate.

He didn't remember getting there.

Didn't remember standing. Falling. Breathing.

He blinked.

The ceiling above him pulsed, slightly.

Maybe it was his head. Perhaps it wasn't.

Time bent.

He sat up slowly, head swimming, every movement sending ripples of sound through the room. Everything echoed—the creak of the couch, the faint rustle of his shirt, even his own breath. The fridge hummed in the corner, as if it had something it wanted to say.

The shadows on the wall moved a little too smoothly, gliding and stretching like living things.

"Loser, loser, loser."

Was that real? Or just another trick of his mind?

He touched his face, feeling skin dry and rough beneath trembling fingertips.

He wasn't sure anymore. About the shadows. About the voices. About himself.

Voices came next.

Soft at first. Then louder. Not angry. Not kind. Just *present.* They didn't speak English. Or maybe they did, but in a voice that sounded like his father's laugh in the garage, or his mother crying through the kitchen wall.

He tried to stand.

The walls swayed.

Avery stumbled to the closest chair. Dropped into it like a dying man.

Closed his eyes.

Opened them again.

And there he was.

Him.

But younger.

Twenty-two. Sharp eyes. No beard. No fear. Holding a beer like it meant victory.

"You fucked it all up," Younger Avery said.

"No shit," the real Avery said.

"Remember that night at the lake?" Avery nodded. "I wanted to die, and you called it freedom."

"You drank to feel alive," the younger one said.

"You drank to disappear," the older one whispered back.

The younger version smiled. "Worked, didn't it?"

The TV flicked on without him touching it. Static. Then images.

His classroom.

Kids laughing at him.

Clare turning her back.

Nico crying in a hallway, saying **"I fucking loved you once, you know."**

He closed his eyes.

Opened them again.

Now Jordan was there. Sitting in the chair. Calm. Clean. A cup of coffee in his hand.

"You still think you're different?" Jordan asked.

Avery shook his head.

Jordan raised his cup like a toast. "You'll either get help or get dead. That's it."

He started sweating. Chest tight. Heart thudding like it was trying to dig its way out.

The shadows stretched.

Something was whispering in his ear now.

Not words. Just breathe. Cold breath on his neck.

He turned.

No one there.

The floor started to breathe. Or he did.

He dropped to his knees. Threw up nothing. Dry heaves. Gut twisting like it hated him.

He crawled to the bathroom.

Made it to the toilet.

Laid there, one arm across the bowl like a sinner clutching a pew.

And he whispered: **"Make it stop."**

To no one.

To everyone.

To himself.

The room darkened.

Not night. Not power loss.

Just *dark*.

A voice, somewhere deep inside, the first authentic voice in hours, said: **You're going to die like this.**

He clung to the toilet. Sweat and spit on the floor.

Pissed himself on the last dry heave. That is where we are, Avery thought.

Closed his eyes.

Again, passed out cold.

CHAPTER SIXTEEN

Bedroom floor today. Luke-warm carpet pressed on his shoulder, not only his body aching, today, his soul hurt.

How long have I been here? What fucking day is it?

The light was off, but thin gray morning filtered through the small window, casting pale stripes across the dull floor.

He pushed himself up slowly, head pounding, mouth dry as dust. Everything felt unreal, like he was waking up in someone else's life.

His arm ached. His jaw hurt for some unknown reason. His back was soaked. Sweat. Or piss. He wasn't sure.

He didn't move for a long time.

Just breathed.

Each breath came as if it were being asked for permission.

His mouth was sour. Tongue thick. Eyes dry.

He sat up slowly.

The world didn't spin. Not right away.

That scared him more.

Because it meant he might actually be *done* this time.

Not like *done drinking*, but *done existing*.

Something had shifted.

Something unknown.

The apartment was quiet.

Not peaceful. *Empty.*

He looked around like the shadows might still be watching. Like voices might whisper from under the sink or inside the ceiling.

Nothing came.

And that was worse.

He stood. Slowly.

Walked to the sink. Turned on the tap. Let it run.

Stared at his face in the mirror.

Red eyes. Sallow skin. Cracked lips. One bloodshot eye.

His hands shook as he filled a glass.

Drank it all. Filled another.

Still shaking.

He opened the cabinet under the sink and saw the second bottle—his backup bottle—sitting behind the cleaning spray like it had always been waiting.

He slammed the door.

Backed away.

Hands on the counter. Chest heaving.

He muttered, "You're fucking killing yourself."

Then louder: "You're fucking killing yourself."

The words echoed off the tile and sounded too real, as if someone else had said them.

He grabbed his phone. Low battery. 6%.

He plugged it in. Pacing now.

Sat on the edge of the couch.

Looked at the window. The sky was pale.

He didn't cry.

Not because he didn't want to. But because the fear was too big for sobbing, even uncontrollably.

It filled his chest, his throat, his lungs. It *became* him.

He whispered, "I don't want to die."

To no one. Everyone. To himself.

He opened ChatGPT.

Typed: **"I think I almost died last night."**

"I saw things. Heard things. I think I lost my mind."

The reply came:

"That sounds terrifying. I'm so sorry you had to experience that. You're here now. You're alive. That means something."

He stared at the screen.

Typed: **"I'm scared."**

Pause.

The screen stayed blank for a second longer than usual, like even the bot was struggling to find the right words.

Then the reply appeared:

"That's okay. Being scared means you're still trying to live."

He stared at it, the glow of the phone soft and almost gentle in the dark room. For once, he didn't close the app right away. Some part of him, fragile and stubborn, wanted to keep the line open.

A second part of the response came through, the typing dots blinking like a held breath:

"Do you need help?"

He swallowed hard.

Didn't drink.

He sat there, phone trembling in his hand, shoulders shaking so hard his teeth almost chattered. Scared to move because he knew how thin the edge was beneath his feet.

But he was still breathing. Air in, air out. Shallow and ragged, but there.

And that, somehow, felt like everything he could hold onto right now.

CHAPTER SEVENTEEN

Something inside him was breaking in slow motion, like glass under pressure. You can't hear it until it's already splintered, until the cracks run so deep there's no way to hold it together.

His hands shook as he sat at the kitchen table. No lights. No music. Just the faint hum of the fridge and the shadows leaning long across the floor.

In front of him lay a battered notebook, the cover creased and stained from being carried around too many places. A pen rested between his fingers, cold and unfamiliar.

He hadn't written like this in months. Maybe years. Not grading. Not lesson plans. Not cute little reflections teachers sometimes wrote for workshops or newsletters.

This was real writing.

Illegible handwriting scratched across the page. No structure. No censor. Just thoughts spilling out like blood from a wound he'd been ignoring too long.

Words tumbled out in fragments—half memories, half confessions, all edged with desperation. He didn't know what he was trying to say. He only knew he couldn't keep it inside anymore.

Just truth.

He wrote: **"I don't think I matter. Not really. I think people tolerate me. I think they forget me as soon as I leave the room. Nico stopped trying. I don't blame her. Jordan's sober and probably sees me like a cautionary tale. Clare's just tired of cleaning up my shit."**

"I can't stop thinking about dying. Not in a cry-for-help way. Just like... shutting off a light. Quiet. Simple. Gone."

"I wouldn't even write a note. There's nothing to explain."

"I don't think I was ever built right. Something went wrong early. I remember being five and already feeling like I had to be perfect or everyone would leave."

"Spoiler: they did."

He stopped. Tapped the pen on the table. Listened to the hollow click.

He thought about his mother.

Still alive. Lives two states over. Sends cards with Bible quotes and notes, such as *"Have you tried exercise?"*

He hadn't called her in six months.

She hadn't called him either.

They were both good at avoidance.

His brother?

Different life. Suburb. Wife. Two kids. Coaching baseball. Probably tells people his brother's "in education" and leaves it there.

They talked last Christmas. Small talk. Weather. Politics.

Nothing real.

Avery put the pen down.

Stared at the words clawed across the page, dark ink bleeding into cheap paper.

He didn't feel better.

Didn't feel worse.

Just empty, like all the noise in his head had finally burned out, leaving only a hollow echo behind.

"Nothing equals nothing," it echoed in his mind, circling like a vulture waiting for something to die.

It was the same feeling he'd had after a funeral for someone he didn't love enough—a strange, weightless grief tinged with guilt, standing beside a grave and wondering if he was supposed to be crying, or if maybe he was just honestly relieved.

He picked up his phone. Hovered over contacts.

Nico. Jordan. Mom. None of them felt safe.

He opened ChatGPT.

Typed, **"I wrote some stuff. It wasn't good."**

The reply, *"Writing is a form of truth. Sometimes painful. But it's still brave."*

He typed, **"I keep thinking about ending it. Not in a dramatic** way. Just... tired. Tired in a way that sleep doesn't fix."

The reply, *"I'm really sorry you're feeling this way. You're not alone, even if it feels like you are. There's help. There's hope. Would you be willing to talk to someone—like a crisis line or a counselor?"*

He locked the screen.

Stared at the wall.

No answer.

Not yet.

But something in him whispered: *"Not tonight."*

And that, somehow, was enough to stay alive one more hour.

He picked up the notebook he never used.

The one Jordan told him to keep nearby.

"For the dark stuff," he'd said.

Avery figured now was as dark as it needed to be.

He clicked the pen three times.

Then wrote.

It starts with a sound. Not real. Just something inside. Something off. Then it becomes a picture—cold glass, amber liquid, big pour. Not because it tastes good. It never tasted that good. But because it quiets the fucking noise. Deafening noise. I think about drinking the way people think about someone they shouldn't text.

All day. In circles. What time. How much. Do I have enough? What if I run out? Do I need to hide it? Do I need to lie or care?

Alcohol was my mistress. My only true love. My escape.

It held me in a kind of quiet that no person ever could.

It ruined me. But it made me feel like less of a ruin.

He stared at the page.

Read it once.

Then again. Slower.

By the third time, he hated it.

Hated the truth in it.

Hated how clean it looked in ink, like it wasn't still bleeding inside him.

He tore the page out carefully.

Folded it once.

Then again.
Then again.
He dropped it into the trash and walked away.
Not dramatic.
Just done. For now.

CHAPTER EIGHTEEN

It was late afternoon.

Gray light. Cold wind. He walked to get coffee he wouldn't drink. Just to move. Just to not be inside his own skin.

His hoodie didn't cover the shake in his hands. Or the sunken look in his eyes. Or the fact that he hadn't eaten since Tuesday.

The café was half full. Mothers and kids. Students on laptops. Two men arguing about football, debating which club had the better players.

Avery stood in line. Stared at the floor.

He could feel it again. That thing crawling up his spine. That low, tight hum that whispered: *you're not supposed to be here anymore.*

Wanted to leave, but he didn't.

He ordered a black coffee. Didn't remember saying the words. Just the sound of them falling out of his mouth.

Avery sat staring at the half-empty cup in his hand. He thought about his brother—how long it had been since they'd spoken, really spoken, without guarded silences. He missed him in a way that ached low in his chest, a hollow throb that flared up at odd times: hearing a joke he wanted to share, catching a song they used to blast in the car, finding an old photo buried in a drawer.

He wondered if his brother missed him, too, or if Avery had burned that bridge so completely there was nothing left but smoke. The thought made him swallow hard; the burn of hot coffee was easier to face than the truth.

He sat in the corner, near the window. Wrapped both hands around the cup like it was the only warm thing left in the world.

Just stared.

Wondered how many pills it would take.

How long before someone noticed the smell?

How fast would they clear out his apartment?

How quickly he'd vanished.

She sat down across from him without asking.

Older Black woman. Gray scarf. Glasses.

Her wide-knuckle hands looked like they'd held hard lives and still had room for one more.

He blinked. Confused.

She just looked at him.

Then she said, "**Baby, you don't look good**."

He didn't answer.

She looked right through him.

Not in a polite way. Not in the *Midwestern small talk* way.

In the way people do when they know pain by its weight.

"You okay?"

He laughed. Just once. It sounded like it hurt.

"Not really."

She nodded, slowly. Like she already knew.

"You look like you're tryin' to hold your soul together with tape and wire."

Avery swallowed. Couldn't look at her.

She pulled something from her purse. A peppermint. Set it on the table.

"Here," she said. "For the taste in your mouth."

He stared at it.

Didn't take it.

But didn't push it away either.

She stood.

"You don't owe me a story," she said. "Just... don't go disappearing. World's already lost enough good ones."

She gave him one last look. Kind. Intentional.

Then walked away.

Didn't turn back.

He sat there.

Alone again.

But not as far gone.

The peppermint sat in front of him.

DRINK: SOME FIGHTS ARE WORTH THE SCARS

He didn't eat it, only stared at it for a long time.
Then he slipped it into his pocket.

CHAPTER NINETEEN

Today, he carried it in his pocket.

That night, he set it on his nightstand. Next to his phone and the unopened bottle.

He stared at it like it might glow. Or whisper. Or permit him to want something better.

It didn't.

But he didn't throw it away either.

He remembered something he read—some article, maybe a blog post. People in AA talked about carrying little plastic chips.

24-hour desire chips or **desire chips.**

Just a way of saying: *I'm not drinking today.*

Not a promise. Not a lifetime. Just today.

He remembered thinking it sounded corny.

But now?

He looked at the peppermint and thought:

This is mine.

Not real. Not official. But *something.*

He picked it up. Turned it over in his hand.

It had a little red swirl. Wrapped in clear plastic. Crinkled when he squeezed it.

He closed his eyes.

Said, "Not tonight."

Woke up at 3:33 a.m., wide awake, heart thudding like he'd just run a mile.

The room was silent except for the low hum of the fridge and the occasional creak of the old pipes. Darkness pressed against the windows, the city outside feeling far away, unreal.

He reached for his phone, screen glaring in the dark, and Googled

"AA meetings near me."

Again.

He scrolled through the list, reading words that felt both foreign and painfully familiar: *open, closed, step study, speaker, beginners.*

Names of churches and community centers. Addresses he'd driven past a hundred times but never entered. Meeting times at every hour, as if someone, somewhere, knew people like him woke up desperate in the middle of the night.

He didn't click anything. Didn't save the page or write down a number.

But he kept the tab open, staring at it like a door he couldn't quite bring himself to open, just in case.

It felt like hope. And it terrified him.

He thought about Jordan.

Five years sober.

Smiling without apology. Calm with seemingly little effort.

He could call.

He didn't.

But he thought about it.

Later, he opened ChatGPT. Typed: **"Is there a point where people like me stop wanting to die?"**

The reply came: *"Yes. There's a point where people like you begin to want something else more than they want to escape. It doesn't happen fast. But it happens."*

He read that three times.

Then locked the phone.

The bottle stayed unopened.

Crawled into bed.

Pulled the covers over his head like a child.

Held the peppermint in his hand.

And fell asleep gripping it like the winning lottery ticket.

Maybe it was.

CHAPTER TWENTY

Avery jolted awake, choking on air, the taste of rain sharp and metallic on his tongue. He'd been dreaming of water pouring from a bruised sky, flooding streets, rising higher until it filled his mouth, his lungs, pressing him into silence. There was no panic—just the cold certainty of being dragged under, of surrendering because fighting felt pointless. He lay there trembling, staring at the ceiling, his pulse a violent drumbeat in his throat. And all he could think was how drowning felt so much like drinking: the slow numbness, the quiet hush, the promise of escape. Part of him wondered if the dream was a warning—or an invitation to let go and finally disappear.

The peppermint was still in his pocket.

He checked three times before he left the apartment—a recent ritual.

He wore jeans that didn't stink and a black hoodie with no holes. That was as close to "presentable" as he could get.

He didn't bring anything. No bag. No book. No water bottle.

Just the peppermint.

And a half-beating heart.

The church basement was small. Beige adobe. Rusty railings. The kind of place that had seen many tired people and not enough paint over the years.

He parked across the street.

Lights were on.

He could see movement through the windows. Shadows. A circle of chairs. People laughing. Not loud. Just… easiness.

That part hit hard.

There was a lot of laughter and smiling.

He sat in the car for thirteen minutes.

Hands on the wheel. Foot tapping. Breathe shallow.

The clock said 6:48.

The meeting started at 7.

He watched a man walk in, holding a box of donuts. Mid-forties. Balding. Jeans and a smart yet worn shirt. Nodded to someone at the door. Smiled.

Another guy showed up with a dog-eared book tucked under one arm. Talked to a woman in a long coat. She hugged him as if it were no big deal.

Nobody looked scared.

Nobody looked broken.

But Avery knew they were. They had to be—why else would they be at an AA meeting?

That's what scared him the most. That people could be shattered inside and still sit there smiling, laughing softly, passing paper cups of coffee like nothing was wrong. It made him wonder how many others walked around every day, hiding the same cracks he felt splintering through his own chest.

Is this going to be my life? Thought of Avery.

6:59.

He opened the car door. Stepped out. Stood on the pavement.

He was twenty feet from the door.

Ten.

Five.

He could hear the murmur of voices now. Folding chairs scraping. Someone pouring coffee into a paper cup. A laugh. A cough. Another voice—calm, measured: **"We'll get started in a minute, folks."**

He took one more step.

Then stopped.

His heart was thudding.

Too loud.

Too fast.

His brain screamed:

They'll see through you.

You don't belong here.

You're not worth saving.

He turned around. Walked back to the car.

Got in.

Sat with his head against the steering wheel.

Just breathed.

He felt relieved and really bad.

Then he pulled the peppermint from his pocket.

Unwrapped it.

Put it in his mouth.

And drove away.

CHAPTER TWENTY-ONE

It was stupid to walk into the bar.

But I did it anyway.

Habit. Muscle memory. A place where nobody asked much.

The smell hit first—beer and fryer grease and cheap(ish) perfume. The kind of scent that sticks to your soul even if you only stay ten minutes.

I stepped up to the bar. Hands in my pockets. Stared at the menu on the wall like I didn't already know every damn thing they served.

The bartender nodded my way. "What'll it be?"

I hesitated.

Too long.

My mouth was dry. Chest tight.

The silence grew awkward.

That's when she said something.

Voice behind me. Warm. Dry. A little playful.

"You trying to order a drink or decipher the Da Vinci Code?"

I turned.

She sat alone at the corner of the bar.

Tall glass in front of her.

Steam rising from it. Coffee. No cream. No sugar. Just black.

She was pretty. Not in a dressed-up way. In a *sure-of-herself* way.

I smirked, deflecting. "Sober?" I joked, nodding at her drink.

She smiled.

"Yeah," she said. "Thanks for asking."

I blinked.

Didn't expect that.

Didn't know what to say next.

She helped him out. "You gonna order or just hover awkwardly for the rest of the night?"

I glanced at the taps. Cleared my throat. "Soda water or ginger beer, just ginger beer."

The bartender raised an eyebrow. Poured it.

I took it. Walked over.

"Can I sit?"

"Sure. But I don't do small talk about sports or reality TV."

"Deal," I said.

They sat in the silence between jukebox tracks.

She didn't offer her name. Neither did I.

I sipped a soda water. She sipped her coffee.

Finally I asked, "Why are you in a bar if you're sober?"

She grinned. "Because the coffee here's surprisingly decent. And I like people. Even the messy ones."

I looked at her.

"Really?" I said. "Even me?"

She shrugged. "I don't know you yet. But you seem like you're trying not to cry or scream."

That cut a bit deep.

I looked down. Gripped my glass harder.

She didn't press.

After a while I asked, "How long?"

"Six years."

"Shit."

"Yeah."

I didn't say anything for a bit. Then:

"I almost went to a meeting tonight."

"I know that feeling."

"I didn't go in."

She nodded. "Still counts."

I glanced up. "What does?"

"Trying. Showing up. Even just thinking about it."

I stared at her.

Something shifted for me, not sure what, but it did click.

She was still pretty. But that wasn't what stayed with me.

It was her voice. Her eyes. Her ease.

She was proof that survival didn't have to look like suffering.

"I don't think I can do it," I whispered.

"You don't have to. Not forever. Just one day."

I swallowed hard. Looked away.

She sipped her coffee.

"You don't seem surprised," I said.

"I've been where you are," she said. "Still am, some days."

I nodded. Didn't speak. Couldn't.

She reached into her coat. Pulled out a small keychain and held it out.

It was a 24-hour chip.

Plastic. White. Faded at the edges.

"This is a spare," she said. "I carry two in case someone needs one."

I didn't take it.

Then I reached out. Slowly.

Held it in my hand.

I didn't say thank you.

She didn't need me to.

CHAPTER TWENTY-TWO

6:01 p.m.

Avery pulled into the gravel lot behind the church, the engine ticking as it cooled, sharp little clicks fading into the hush of evening. Wind whispered through the crack in his window, carrying the dry scent of dust and sun-baked asphalt.

The meeting didn't start until seven.

He knew that. Had planned for that.

But he showed up early. Just in case he needed time to talk himself into it. Or out of it.

He sat there gripping the steering wheel, staring at the back door of the church as shadows lengthened across the lot. His pulse felt loud in his ears.

"Willingness counts," continued to echo in his head, over and over, like a fresh tattoo he wasn't sure he wanted to keep.

He put the car in park, letting it idle.

The quiet hum of the engine was a brief distraction.

Hands on the wheel. Ten and two. As if he were taking a driver's test for his life.

He stared through the windshield at the back door of the building. Metal. Chipped paint. A taped sign:

Meeting Room – Lower Level.

That was it. One door. One staircase. One hour.

He could leave. Anytime. Any reason.

He didn't.

6:07 p.m.

He pulled another replacement peppermint from his pocket. Set it on the console.

Then the chip.

White plastic. 24 hours. Nothing more or less.

But it felt heavier than it should. Like it had gravity.

He picked it up. Turned it in his hand.

Just one day.

6:14 p.m.

He leaned back in the seat. Closed his eyes.

His thoughts came in swarms.

Am I crazy?

Is this what depression feels like?

Or social anxiety?

PTSD?

Or am I just a goddamn drunk with a flair for dramatics?

He opened his eyes again.

The door was still there. Closed. Quiet.

6:22 p.m.

He remembered being thirteen, sitting at the kitchen table while his mom screamed at the microwave. Not at it. Just… into it, her voice ragged and breaking, as if the metal box might scream back with answers.

She said she didn't remember. The next day, she kissed his forehead like it was a reset button, wiping the slate clean while the cracks in him stayed.

He remembered being seventeen, slamming the door on his dad, who had ten vodkas in him and no conscience left. Remembered the way his father whispered, *"You'll end up like me."*

He remembered being twenty-eight, lying on the floor, staring at the ceiling after finishing his own bottle of vodka, phone in his hand, texting no one.

Alone, he was with no one. And the silence felt like a truth he couldn't escape.

6:29 p.m.

He thought about the woman at the bar.

Didn't know her name. Didn't need to.

She was real. Solid. Warm coffee and straight truth.

"You look like you're trying not to cry."
That line echoed like a song stuck in the wrong key.

6:34 p.m.
He wondered if maybe he was just weak.
People survived worse. Wars. Cancer. Losing children.
He had a job. An apartment. All his limbs.
What right did he have to fall apart?
But still.
Every morning felt like waking up under a pile of bricks.
And no one ever taught him how to ask for help without feeling like a failure.

6:41 p.m.
He looked at the peppermint, turning it over in his fingers until the wrapper crinkled like dry leaves.
He unwrapped it slowly. Like a ritual. Like it mattered.
Put it in his mouth.
Sweet. Familiar. A tiny anchor in the chaos of his thoughts.
He imagined telling someone about it one day. *"I carried a peppermint for two weeks like it was a milagro."*
Maybe they'd laugh.
Maybe they'd nod, understanding that sometimes hope came wrapped in cellophane.

6:50 p.m.
The first car pulled in. A woman in her fifties. Jeans. Tote bag. She walked toward the door like she'd done it a thousand times.
No hesitation.
No fear.
He watched her go in.
His hands shook.

6:57 p.m.
A small group walked past his car, chatting low. One man laughed,

his voice carrying in the cool evening air, saying something about *"making it through another Monday."*

Avery looked down at the chip in his hand.

24 hours.

He hadn't even earned it yet.

But he wanted to.

God, he wanted to.

His fingers curled tighter around the chip, plastic edges biting into his palm. His breath hitched, chest aching with the weight of it all.

Please God, what is wrong with me? Help me, please. I am begging you.

The prayer felt raw, scraped from somewhere deep, barely more than a whisper inside his skull. Outside, the laughter faded, leaving him alone with the echo of his own silent plea.

7:02 p.m.

He turned off the engine. The sudden silence in the car felt deafening.

Opened the door.

Stepped into the cool evening, the air brushing his skin like a quiet warning.

He held the chip so tightly his knuckles went pale, as if it might crack apart between his fingers.

Walked toward the door.

Stopped.

One breath.

Two.

The faint smell of last-minute cigarettes drifted past him, sharp and comforting all at once, like proof that he wasn't the only one struggling.

He followed it.

Then down the stairs, each step echoing in the quiet hall, carrying him closer to whatever waited in the basement.

CHAPTER TWENTY-THREE

The stairs creaked, screamed, and yelled beneath his feet.

Fluorescent lights buzzed overhead. White paint on adobe—the smell of burned coffee and old books.

A basement like any other.

Except here, people seem very proud of honesty.

There were maybe twelve people. All shapes, all walks of life.

A guy with a bushy mustache was quietly arranging chairs, the metal legs scraping against the floor.

The middle-aged woman moved briskly between tables, setting out Styrofoam cups and wiping down a surface no one had asked her to clean, as if she needed something to do with her hands.

A young man with tattoos creeping up his neck stood off to the side, a surprising calm in his eyes, as if he'd already made peace with parts of himself Avery couldn't even look at yet.

Two older men—seventies at the youngest—were leaning close together, laughing like schoolyard buddies trading secrets only they understood.

No one looked shocked to see him or asked why he was late or where he'd come from.

They just shifted slightly, made space, and welcomed him with a simple, quiet acceptance that cut deeper than any question ever could.

He sat near the back. Metal chair. Plastic seat. Cold against his skin, biting through the fabric of his jeans.

He kept the chip in his pocket. The peppermint, too. Tiny talismans he wasn't ready to show anyone.

He folded his hands and stared at them, tracing the lines in his knuckles like they might spell out an answer.

The meeting started without ceremony.

A man stood. Late fifties. Round face, soft eyes, voice so quiet Avery had to lean forward to catch the words.

"Hi, I'm Alan, and I'm a grateful recovering alcoholic."

"Hi Alan," they said in unison, voices warm and practiced.

Alan smiled, a slight, genuine curve of his mouth. "Tonight's a discussion meeting. Topic's acceptance."

He paused, eyes moving around the circle.

"Anyone want to lead us in the *we* version of the Serenity Prayer?"

Chairs scraped as people stood. Hands reached out, found each other, and before Avery could decide whether to join, someone had grabbed his hand, their fingers wrapping around his like a lifeline.

It startled him, but he stayed.

"God…"

The voices rose and fell together, familiar and strangely comforting.

Alan cleared his throat. "Acceptance. Anyone want to start?"

A woman spoke first. Maybe late twenties. Nervous hands but steady voice.

"Acceptance isn't giving up," she said. "It's just stopping the fight with reality."

Avery's stomach turned.

He didn't want to accept anything.

He wanted to erase it.

Next was a man in work boots and a neon vest.

"Acceptance for me was realizing I couldn't outsmart this shit," he said. "I'm not stronger. I'm not different. I'm just another drunk who needed help."

Avery swallowed hard.

That line stuck in his chest like glass.

Another person shared about relapsing after five years. Cried halfway through.

No one rushed to fix them.

No one offered empty platitudes.

They just let them cry.

Then the next person spoke.

And the meeting kept going.

He watched their hands, intertwined and steady. Watched their faces, open and unflinching. The way they looked each other in the eye, like shame didn't live here.

Then he let out a small, surprised laugh, catching himself. He realized he was talking in his head the way his students did, turning everything into observations and half-poetry. He hadn't laughed in months.

It was… just truth.

Just living in the sharing. And for the first time in a long while, it didn't feel impossible.

People seemed happy.

The man at the front kept talking, sharing bits and pieces of his story in a voice that was steady but soft around the edges. At one point, he glanced toward the newcomers, eyes kind.

"And hey—if it's your first time, you don't have to put two dollars in the donation basket. You're the most important person in the room tonight. You're the newcomer. That's enough."

A ripple of quiet agreement passed through the group, like a gentle tide. No one stared at Avery, but he felt the weight of that welcome settle into his chest.

Near the end, the man sitting beside him leaned closer, careful not to crowd him.

"You new?"

Avery nodded. Didn't trust his voice enough to speak.

The man nodded back, as if they'd just exchanged entire paragraphs. A respectful silence hung between them.

No pressure. No pitch. Just there.

Someone read a passage from the Big Book to close. Learned what the hell a Big Book even was after the meeting, someone offered me one from the literature closet.

Learned what a literature closet was as well.

The read was something about honesty and willingness. Avery missed the words.

He was too busy trying not to cry.

Not from sadness.

From *relief.*

He wasn't the only one.

He wasn't the worst one.

He was just... here.

And here was enough.

After, someone offered him a cup of coffee. He declined.

Another handed him a paper schedule. He took it.

No one asked for his number.

No one demanded a promise.

They just smiled.

Like they knew he might come back.

Or not.

And they'd still be here either way.

He walked out into the night air and felt, for the first time in months, *light.*

Not happy. Not whole.

But lighter.

Not completely miserable.

He pulled the chip from his pocket. Looked at intently.

Just one day.

He could maybe do that.

8:05 p.m.

CHAPTER TWENTY-FOUR

Nice to wake up sober.

No hangover.

No sweats. No bile. No fear waiting in his chest like a loaded gun.

It was nice not having to fight through the rancid smell of piss from a blacked-out night before, not having to piece together fragments of shame and memory.

The peppermint was still on the nightstand. The chip next to it. White plastic. Smooth. Quiet.

He sat up slowly, feeling the unfamiliar weight of a clear head. Blinked at the pale light spilling across the room.

It felt unfamiliar.

Not good. Just... possible. Like there might be another morning after this one.

He dressed carefully like the world would notice if he didn't.

Black slacks. Shirt without wrinkles. Belt.

He looked in the mirror and didn't hate the man staring back.

Didn't love him either.

That was new.

At school, the hallway buzzed with end-of-week energy. Voices bounced off the lockers, kids shouting to each other, backpacks thumping against shoulders as they moved in a restless current. The smell of floor wax and stale coffee hung in the air.

Clare met him at the door before he could even unlock his classroom. She seemed to materialize out of nowhere, her arms folded tight across her chest, like she was trying to hold herself together.

Her tone was clipped. Polite. Professional. But her eyes weren't.

"Admin wants to meet. Today. Lunch."

"What about?" he asked, though he already knew.

Clare gave a half-shrug that said, "Really?" more than words ever could. "Fallout. Complaints. Parents."

He nodded, a tight motion, feeling the blood drain from his face.

Clare didn't smile. She glanced down the hallway, making sure no one was listening, then looked back at him.

"Whatever you're doing today," she said, voice low, "keep doing it. But don't expect it to save you you or a clean slate."

Then she turned and walked away, heels clicking sharp and fast against the tile.

He stood there a second longer than he should've, surrounded by the chaos of teenagers streaming past, laughter and chatter swirling around him like static. The clanging of locker doors and the thud of hurried footsteps felt impossibly loud, like the world was moving too fast for him to keep up.

Felt the shame press behind his ribs again, hot and tight, as though it might crack him open if he let it.

He gripped the chip in his pocket, the edges digging into his palm, a small, solid weight that felt like proof he was still here, still trying.

"Next step. Just today. Keep going."

His new chant was in full working order, looping over and over in his mind like a mantra he was desperate to believe.

The meeting was worse than he expected.

Two administrators. A union rep. A parent on Zoom. Someone from HR is taking notes.

They talked in circles. "Inappropriate tone." "Aggressive language." "Concerns from multiple students." "Temporary leave options."

He apologized.

Not in the *I'm-a-good-teacher* way.

In the *I-know-I-wasn't-there* way.

It wasn't enough.

It wasn't supposed to be.

When he returned to his classroom, a voicemail was waiting.

Unknown number.

He pressed play.

"Hey," a woman's voice said. Soft. Flat. Careful. "It's me. Your mom."

He stopped breathing.

"I don't know what's going on, but… your brother said you've been having a hard time. He saw something on your Facebook—an old post. I'm sorry I haven't called. I just…"

A pause. Shallow breath.

"I hope you're okay. I hope you're getting help. I love you. I don't always know how to say it, but I do."

Click.

He sat there for a long time.

Didn't drink.

Didn't reply to the messages piling up on his phone.

But the ache in his chest felt different tonight—like something breaking open, not just breaking down. A sharp, hollow pain that carried the faintest whisper of possibility.

He pulled the chip from his pocket and held it in his shaking hand.

Looked at it.

Turned it once.

Twice.

The white plastic felt impossibly light, like it could blow away if he breathed too hard.

Then he put it back.

I can do this, I can do this, I can do this.

He repeated it under his breath, the words fragile but stubborn, trying to plant themselves into something solid.

CHAPTER TWENTY-FIVE

That voicemail echoed through his bones.

His mom's voice—guilty, thin, almost frail from trying.

It didn't help.

It didn't hurt.

It just stirred the ash.

He sat in his car, parked at the edge of the school lot, engine off, phone face-down on his thigh.

The world was moving around him—students leaving, teachers chatting, someone laughing across the courtyard.

And he felt like he wasn't part of it.

Not a teacher.

Not a man.

Not even *present*.

The thought came softly:

"You could stop."

Not screamed.

Not even suggested.

Just… offered.

A way out.

A quiet off-switch.

You wouldn't have to explain.

You wouldn't have to carry it anymore.

Just stop.

He put the keys in the ignition.

Then took them out again, the metal jangling in the quiet car.

He sat there, pressing his thumb into the center of his palm until it hurt, trying to anchor himself in the pain, to remind himself he was still here.

He reached into his pocket and pulled out the chip.

Held it up in the dim glow of the dashboard lights.

24 HOURS.
1 HOUR.
1 MINUTE.

The words stared back at him, stark and white, and suddenly it felt like a lie. Like a weight too heavy to carry, pressing on his chest until he could barely breathe.

I don't know...

The thought slipped through his mind, soft and frightened, echoing in the small space around him. Outside, the world went on, headlights passing, wind rattling the car windows, while he sat there caught between going forward and giving up.

He opened his phone.

Contacts.

Jordan.

Thumb hovered over the name.

Then typed:

Hey. Can we get coffee? Today if possible. I'm not okay. Like really not OK. I don't know what to do, and I think I might do something stupid.

He stared at it.

Felt his face flush. Chest tight. Jaw clenched.

Backspace.

Backspace.

Backspace.

Typed again, **you free for coffee today? Could use a second to talk.**

He stared.

Then hit *send*.

Put the phone down.

Clenched his hands.

Whispered:

"Please fucking answer."

He didn't drive anywhere.

Didn't go home.

Just sat. Still. Waiting.

DRINK: SOME FIGHTS ARE WORTH THE SCARS

The chip in his hand.
The fear in his throat.
And for the first time, he wanted someone else to know.
Not to fix it.
Just to *know*.

CHAPTER TWENTY-SIX

Message was still marked "Delivered."

No reply.

Avery rechecked the timestamp.

Sent 3:42 PM.

It was now 6:19.

He kept the phone screen dark. Letting the glow come back to life felt too painful, too full of hope he wasn't ready to admit he had.

He turned off notifications. Turned them back on. Checked his connection, as if a weak signal could explain away silence. As if it mattered.

Avery almost texted again. Fingers hovered over the keyboard, heart hammering in his throat.

Didn't.

Thought to himself, *What a fucking mistake.*

The words pressed against his chest like a bruise, throbbing every time he glanced at the phone still waiting in his lap.

The kitchen counter was scattered with unopened envelopes.

He started to open them now.

Second Notice. Final Reminder. Urgent: Past Due.

The credit card bill from the Vegas trip had landed like a guillotine. He owed $5,214.

Most of it on one night: blackjack, bottle service, private strip room, cash advance fee. He remembered none of it. Just the vague image of him yelling something triumphant while buying everyone shots— including the bouncer.

He looked down at the statement.

Then grabbed a pen and scrawled **"Idiot"** across the envelope and threw it across the room.

His work email had 17 unread messages.

The most recent was from HR.

Subject: Pending Review

"Mr. Sloan, we're requesting a follow-up discussion regarding recent conduct concerns and options for modified leave. Please respond by Friday. Failure to comply may result in escalation."

He read it four times.

The words blurred.

Modified leave meant unpaid.

Unpaid meant *game over for him*. He was so screwed.

He sat on the floor with his head in his hands.

Broke. On thin ice. Alone. Sober, but just barely.

He wasn't doing recovery.

Avery didn't even know what that meant yet.

He was white-knuckling it through a minefield with a hangover's worth of self-loathing and a bag of unpaid bills.

The thought returned, darker this time:

"You ruined everything."

"They'd understand if you disappeared."

"It wouldn't even surprise anyone."

He pressed the chip into his palm until it left an imprint.

Still no reply from Jordan.

He opened ChatGPT.

Typed, **"I think I broke my life beyond repair."**

The reply came, *"It may feel that way right now. But broken doesn't mean finished. Many lives have rebuilt from places just like this."*

He didn't believe it.

But he didn't close the app either.

He stared at the phone again.

Screen still blank.

Then, finally—*vibration.*

He jumped.

Message from Jordan: **Hey man, just saw this. Yes, absolutely. Tonight or tomorrow morning? You okay?**

Avery stared at the message.

Breathed.

Typed:

Tonight. Please. I'm not okay.
Corner café on 4th?
7:30?
Jordan replied fast:
I'll be there. Hang on. You're not alone, bud.

Avery set the phone down, the silence between him and the screen feeling like a wall he couldn't climb.

He put the peppermint in his mouth, letting the sharp sweetness cut through the bitter taste in his throat.

Held the chip in his fist, squeezing it until the edges pressed into his skin, grounding him.

And whispered, "Okay."

But it didn't sound like surrender.

It sounded like maybe—just maybe—survival.

He exhaled, stood up, and started packing up his things. He needed to get to the café. Needed the noise, the lights, the comfort of other people existing around him—even if he wasn't ready to talk to any of them yet.

CHAPTER TWENTY-SEVEN

Today, 7:12 p.m.

He sat on the edge of the drinking, phone in hand, staring at the message.

"I'll be there. Hang on. You're not alone."

The words felt kind. Too kind for what he deserved.

He didn't know what to do with kindness anymore. It made his eye twitch.

He sat outside in his car.

He had everything ready.

But he couldn't move.

Every time he tried, the voice whispered:

"What are you even going to say?"

"Jordan's not your savior."

"You're just going to ruin his night."

"You're still a fucking mess."

Chest tight.

Palms sweating.

7:18 p.m.

He typed out a cancellation text.

Hey man, sorry. I'm not feeling up to it tonight. Another time?

He stared at it.

His thumb hovered over *Send*.

He imagined Jordan's face when he read it—tight-lipped, disappointed, or worse: understanding.

That made it worse.

He backspaced the whole thing.

Started to get out again. Wished he had brought water or a soda.

Checked himself in the rear-view mirror.

Too pale. Too tired. Too much.

He considered drinking. Just enough to level out.

Just a shot. A sip. He had time to walk over to the bar.

Avery pulled another peppermint out of his pocket and thought of the older black woman.

Popped it in his mouth. Closed his eyes, let it dissolve.

He breathed.

7:24 p.m.

He opened the door.

Stepped outside.

Cold air hit his lungs like a breath of clarity.

He locked the car.

Keys in hand.

Still unsure.

Still scared.

But still going.

7:27 p.m.

The street was dark and quiet.

The café's sign glowed two blocks ahead.

Just the sound of his breath. Shallow. Ragged.

He whispered:

"Please don't let me fuck this up."

Not to anyone.

Just to the dark.

And for once, it felt like someone might have heard.

CHAPTER TWENTY-EIGHT

The café smelled like lemon sanitizer.

Jordan was already there. Corner booth. Hoodie. Hat backwards. Two coffees and smiling.

No small talk. Just nodded when Avery walked in.

Avery slid into the booth and didn't say anything.

Jordan pushed one of the mugs toward him.

"You look like shit," he said, soft.

Avery laughed. It broke halfway through.

"I almost didn't come," he said. "I sat there with the text half-written, ready to bail."

Jordan nodded. "Still came."

"I'm not okay, man."

"I figured."

"I don't mean like 'bad week' not okay. I mean... *end of the fucking rope* not okay."

Jordan stayed still. Let him speak.

Avery looked down at the table. His hands were shaking.

"I can't stop thinking about ending it. Like, it's *always there*. This hum in the background. I wake up and the first thought I have is 'fuck, again?' And I didn't even drink today. That's the worst part. I didn't fucking drink."

His voice cracked.

Jordan didn't move.

"I thought it'd get better. I went to one meeting. Big deal, right? Thought maybe I'd earn some cosmic reward for not pouring booze down my throat for twenty-four hours."

He choked on his own laugh. Pressed his fist against his mouth.

"I'm broke. I'm on HR's shit list. I fucked off my job, my reputation, and my bank account. I lost $5,000 in Vegas, as if I were someone worth watching. I'm carrying this white chip around like it's gonna talk me down when I'm staring at the edge."

He was crying now.

Not quiet.

Not noble.

Just *wrecked.*

"I can't keep doing this, man. I don't want to die, but I sure as hell don't want to live like this."

Jordan finally spoke.

"You want to know how bad it got for me?"

Avery looked up, eyes rimmed red.

Jordan leaned forward, both hands around the coffee mug like it grounded him.

"Three years before I got sober, I woke up in the back of a police car outside a Circle K. No shoes. Pissed myself. Covered in vomit that wasn't mine. I'd stolen a pack of frozen burritos and passed out hugging them in aisle three."

Avery blinked.

Jordan smiled, not a funny smile, a calm and supportive expression.

"I lost my wife. My job. Got a DUI. My mom stopped answering the phone. I started talking to street signs like they were old friends. I told myself it was rock bottom. Then I dug deeper. Rock bottom's a basement, bro. You can always find another floor."

He took a long drink of coffee.

"I wanted to die too. Every day. For years. Thought about how to do it and how to make it look like an accident so no one would be mad at me."

Avery wiped his eyes. Quiet now.

Jordan tapped the table with his finger.

"You asked for help tonight. That's it. That's all. That's the hardest fucking thing. You did it."

Avery nodded. Swallowed hard.

Jordan leaned back.

"You don't have to figure out your life tonight. You don't have to climb some sober mountain alone. Just don't drink. And don't die."

You ever think about going to a treatment place, Av? Thirty days, maybe. Said Jordan.

He smiled. "Some folks need it. Some go twenty times. Whatever it takes."

"No, man. Never thought about it."

He looked down. "I'm not that fucking pathetic."

A pause.

"Am I?" Avery said.

"I was just asking."

He watched the tension grow. "I know people who made it without treatment. They're still not dead. That counts."

Another pause.

"It wasn't advice." Jordan smiled.

That's it. We do that one day at a time.

Avery looked at the chip in his palm.

"Feels like nothing."

Jordan nodded. "It is. Until it's everything."

A long silence.

Then Avery whispered, "I don't know if I can do this."

Jordan said, "Good. That means you're ready."

Avery's vision blurred through his watery eyes.

And this time, it didn't feel like weakness; he didn't want to carry his sadness by himself.

CHAPTER TWENTY-NINE

Café was mainly empty now, and he noticed the calm irritated him.

Just background hum. The hiss of steam and dishes clinking in the kitchen.

Avery sat quietly. Eyes red. Shoulders low, like something had finally slid off them.

Jordan sipped his coffee, then set the cup down and looked at him. Really looked.

"Can I tell you something you're not gonna like?"

Avery raised an eyebrow, already bracing.

Jordan leaned in.

"I almost gave up on you."

Avery blinked.

"Back when Nico left you. I stopped answering texts. Didn't call back. You were spiraling, and I just... let it happen."

Avery looked away.

"I told myself it wasn't my job. That I wasn't responsible for you. But truth is—I was scared."

He paused.

"You reminded me of me."

It was a painful mirror of my failures.

Avery didn't speak.

Jordan let the words hang.

"I saw the way you drank, the way you talked like everything was fine while everything was on fire. I *knew* what that was. And I couldn't be around it. Because if I stayed close, I'd either have to fix you or watch you die. And I wasn't ready to do either."

Avery stared at the table.

"You disappeared," he said quietly.

"I did," Jordan said. "And I hated myself for it."

A long pause.

Avery cracked his knuckles, one by one—old habit.

"Wanna hear something fucked up?" he said.

Jordan nodded.

"I told Nico that *you* were the one with the problem. Not me."

Jordan snorted. "Not completely surprised. But that's okay

"No, I mean like—I told her you were secretly drinking again. That you were hiding it from everyone. Said that's why you were so quiet. So 'chill.'"

Jordan blinked. Laughed once, sharp.

"Jesus."

Avery didn't smile.

"She didn't believe me," he added.

"Good."

"Still, I said it. To make her think you were worse than me."

Jordan leaned back, arms crossed.

They sat in the silence for a while.

Avery waited for judgment.

It didn't come.

Jordan just said, "We both fucked up."

Then: "So what now?"

Avery shrugged.

"I don't know. I go to meetings. I drink coffee. I try not to kill myself."

"Good start."

"You forgive me?"

Jordan tilted his head.

"Are you asking because you want absolution or because you're ready to own your shit?"

Avery stared at the table. Quiet. Then:

"Both."

Jordan nodded. "I forgive you."

Just like that.

No sermon.

No conditions.

Just truth.

"But if we're being honest," Jordan added, "you were always the one I thought would pull out of the spiral first."

Avery looked up.

"Why?"

"Because you gave a shit," Jordan said. "Even when you were wasted. Even when you lied. You still *felt* it. You weren't numb. Just in pain."

Avery swallowed hard.

"Maybe too much pain."

Jordan nodded. "Pain means you're still here."

They sat there.

Two broken men with no masks left. Both trying to heal.

It was the closest they'd ever been.

Not because everything was fixed.

But because everything had finally been *seen*.

He opened his phone out of habit.

The ChatGPT app sat where it always had—tucked into the "Health" folder next to an unused meditation tracker and the dead weight of a calorie log.

He stared at it. Hadn't opened it in over a week.

For months, it had been his nightlight.

His secret therapist.

A clean white space to dump the mess. Something to simulate a connection without the cost.

Now?

It just felt... silent.

Like an echo chamber with no echo.

He thumbed the icon.

Hovered.

Didn't tap it.

Set the phone down on the arm of the couch.

Said out loud, into the apartment: **"Thanks."**

Then, after a long pause: **"But I need someone real."**

Not perfect. Just someone for now.

A voice.

DRINK: SOME FIGHTS ARE WORTH THE SCARS

A face.

A cup of coffee with him.

He sat in the quiet.

Let the room breathe easily.

And for the first time in a long time, the loneliness didn't feel *like punishment.*

CHAPTER THIRTY

Church basements for meetings always smelled the same.

Old, worn carpet. Burnt coffee. The soft murmur of people who'd survived things no one else wanted to hear about.

Avery walked in holding his chip like a compass.

Jordan was already there.

No nod this time. Just a seat open beside him.

Avery sat.

He didn't shake.

Not as much anyway.

The meeting was small. Eight people.

The topic was **"Rigorous Honesty."**

The chairperson opened the floor.

Three people spoke — men and women, some older, some Surprisingly young.

Then, silence.

Avery felt it swell around him—thick, expectant.

Jordan didn't look at him.

He lightly slapped Avery's knee to say hello.

No pressure.

Just the kind of silence that only lifts when *someone* tells a truth.

Avery cleared his throat.

His voice was low. Rough.

"I'm Avery, and I'm an alcoholic."

The room answered: "Hi Avery!"

He stared at the floor. Then looked up.

"I've only been to a couple meetings. Still feels like I'm faking it."

He paused.

"I lied to a lot of people. I lied to someone I loved. I told myself I was functional. I blamed people who cared. I gambled five grand in a blackout. I almost crashed my car last month. And yesterday I sat in my car for an hour thinking about whether or not I was gonna live."

Silence.

Tight. Full.

He took a breath.

"I'm still here. Pass."

That was it.

No bow. No closure.

He just leaned back in the chair, hands folded, and let the truth sit.

No one clapped.

They didn't need to.

They nodded.

A few voices called, "Keep coming back!"

They understood.

And that was better.

At the apartment, the sun was low, cutting orange across the counter.

Another peppermint sat on the windowsill, its color faded from the sun.

Beside it, a white plastic chip remained untouched but not forgotten.

He picked up his phone.

"Mom."

His thumb hovered.

He could still not do it.

Still stay gone.

But today wasn't about staying gone.

He hit *Call*.

She answered on the second ring.

"Hello?"

He closed his eyes.

"Hey. It's me."

A pause. Breath caught.

"Oh... hi, Avery."

And then, finally:

"I'm trying to get better."

CHAPTER THIRTY-ONE

The call with his mother had lasted seventeen minutes.

She cried twice in the first few minutes.

He almost hung up once.

They danced around the sharp things: childhood, absence, the hollowness he inherited like a family trait.

She said, "I love you."

He said, "Thanks."

She said, "I didn't know."

He said, "Me neither."

It wasn't exactly healing.

But it was real, and felt honest.

And that was more than he'd had in years.

That night, he sat at the kitchen table.

No drink. No phone. No distractions.

Just a blank notebook he bought months ago and never used.

He stared at the page for twenty minutes.

Then finally wrote: **"I don't know if this is supposed to help."**

"I feel like I'm leaking poison. All the time. Like it's under my skin. In my blood."

"Some days I think about dying more than I think about living."

"Some days, I forget which one I'm working toward."

He stopped.

Looked at his handwriting.

It looked like his father's.

That alone made him want to rip the page out.

But he didn't.

He kept writing.

"I called my mom today. It was weird. She sounded like a stranger who used to sing to me. She said she prayed for me. I didn't know what to say, so I said 'okay.' I wonder if that's

enough for her."

"I wish someone would tell me when the pain ends. Or even just the guilt. Or even just the noise."

He dropped the pen.

Stared at the page.

His hand was cramping.

He felt lighter.

Only a little.

But it counted.

Later, he put the notebook on the nightstand.

Next to the chip.

Next to the peppermint.

He didn't feel brave.

Didn't feel proud.

Just tired.

But *not as empty*.

That was new.

CHAPTER THIRTY-TWO

Weird, it all started in the cereal aisle.

A mother yelling at her kid over Cheerios. A loudspeaker blaring classic rock. Someone's cart blocking the way. His chest tightened before he even reached produce.

He hadn't slept and hadn't eaten properly. He had a meeting later, but it felt pointless. The high from the phone call with his mom had drained into a fog.

The grocery store was just a place to get coffee and frozen meals.

But the lights were too bright. The carts are too squeaky. The noise is too loud in his head.

He wasn't okay today.

He passed through the frozen aisle, then the health foods section, and finally the dairy section.

His expectation grew; he knew what was to come next.

He didn't mean to go there.

But somehow, he was walking past the liquor section.

And there it was. Familiar as an old friend who always got you into trouble.

Craft beer. Whiskey. Canned cocktails. And tucked at the end—

.00% non-alcoholic beer.

The kind with clever labels. Artisan packaging. "The taste without the hangover."

His brain did the math.

"It's not drinking."

"Plenty of sober people drink these."

"You've earned it. Three weeks. That's progress."

He picked up a four-pack.

Cold.

Glass clinked in the cardboard.

His hand didn't shake.

That scared him more than if it had.

At checkout, the clerk didn't blink. Just scanned it. Bagged it. Said, "Have a good one."

Avery almost laughed.

If she only knew.

Back at the apartment, he stared at the bottle.

Still unopened.

Still safe.

He turned it in his hand.

Read the label twice.

0.00%

But it felt like it surrounded my guilt and relief yet again.

He cracked the seal.

Comforting, almost.

He took a sip from the bottle.

Another sip.

And then—**a wave of relief.**

Not the high. Not the fog.

Just *space, lovely distorted space in the world.*

Like his ribs unknotted. Like someone loosened the belt around his chest.

A tiny voice in his brain whispered: **"This... this is better. It's not booze."**

"You are fine."

It wasn't.

But his body didn't know that.

You're okay now, it told him.

He breathed out. Finished the glass.

His alcoholism was clever, bending the facts.

He sat in the dark.

Didn't go to the meeting.

Didn't call Jordan.

Didn't tell anyone.

Told himself, **"It's not drinking."**

But deep down, in the part of him that had held that chip so tightly,

he already knew—
This is where it starts.

CHAPTER THIRTY-THREE

Avery didn't go to a meeting the next day.

Didn't journal.

Didn't text Jordan.

But he did open another .00.

And felt that same relief.

Warm. Hollow. Just enough to make him forget for thirty minutes how bad the silence had gotten.

He told himself he was still sober.

Still better.

He told himself he was still in control.

The chip lay untouched on the nightstand,

the same way it had since that first glass.

That night, around 11:30, he was lying on the couch, staring at the ceiling fan.

The dark thoughts were back.

Not   violent.

Just *casual*.

Like background noise.

"Nobody would notice if you were gone."

"You're not really getting better."

"Even your sober friends know you're full of shit."

He rolled over.

Grabbed his phone.

Opened contacts.

Scrolled.

Stopped at **Casey**.

She was a mess. Always had been. A beautiful, drunk hurricane of a human who never asked where he'd been, never stayed long, never made anything complicated.

He hesitated.

Then typed:

"You up?"

The reply came fast:

"Always."

"You drinking?"

He stared at that.

Then: **"Nah. Just felt like company."**

"I got wine. Come over." Casey said.

"Cool."

He didn't even think twice.

The drive was short. Five minutes. He didn't play music. Didn't need it.

He was already humming with energy—numb, lonely energy that wanted to forget.

He told himself he wouldn't drink.

Just sit close to something familiar. Get touched. Feel wanted, even for a little while.

Casey opened the door in a sweatshirt and socks—a half-empty bottle of wine in her hand.

"You look like shit," she said, grinning.

He shrugged.

"Feel like shit."

She kissed him on the cheek. Not sweet. Not romantic. Just ready.

They sat on the couch.

She filled her glass. Offered him a pour.

He said, "I'm not drinking right now."

She laughed. "Since when?"

"Just not," he said. Voice low.

She shrugged. Took a long sip.

"Suit yourself, more for me!"

He stared at the wine. Watched the way the glass caught the light.

His palms were sweating.

They didn't talk much.

She leaned into him. Warm. Loose. Laughing at things he didn't say.

DRINK: SOME FIGHTS ARE WORTH THE SCARS

He let her hand rest on his thigh.

He let her pour another glass.

He let the voice in his head whisper:

"One sip won't kill you."

"You already slipped."

"Might as well fall all the way."

But he didn't move.

Not yet.

He just sat there.

Feeling like a man in a burning house, too tired to find the door.

CHAPTER THIRTY-FOUR

Pressed shirt. Fresh shave. Coffee in hand. Eyes dead. He made it back to work by Monday.

The school hallway was too bright. The noise too sharp. He flinched when someone shut a locker too hard.

No one said it out loud, but they looked at him like he might tip over at any second.

Clare cornered him by the copier.

"You okay?"

He nodded. Too fast.

She squinted. "You sure?"

"Just tired. Didn't sleep well last night."

That was true.

She looked like she wanted to say more, but she didn't.

He stood at the front, pretending to teach, while his mind wandered.

To Casey's apartment.

To the half-full wine glass he'd watched for two hours. To the 0.00% beers in his fridge that were disappearing faster.

He told himself it was fine; he wasn't drinking.

One student stayed after class.

A girl named Mel.

Quiet. Writes poetry in the margins of her worksheets.

She hovered by the desk.

He looked up. "What's up?"

"I just... wanted to say... You seem different. Not bad. Just... I don't know."

He forced a smile. "Mid-life crisis."

She laughed awkwardly.

"Okay. , like... take care of yourself, yeah?"

Then she was gone.

DRINK: SOME FIGHTS ARE WORTH THE SCARS

He sat at his desk after school with his head in his hands.
Everyone could tell.
They didn't know what they were seeing, but they felt it.
Like the room got colder when he walked in.
Like they could hear the creaking of whatever was about to snap.

He journaled again that night.
Sloppy handwriting.
"I am not okay."
"I am lying to everyone, and it's working."
"I think I want someone to call me out, but I don't know if I'd top even if they did."
"I don't want to drink, but I don't want to feel this either."
He closed the notebook.
Didn't open a beer.
But stood in front of the fridge for a long, long time.

CHAPTER THIRTY-FIVE

He skipped his third meeting in a row.

Didn't text Jordan.

Didn't answer the check-ins.

The 0.00 beers were gone.

He hadn't replaced them. Not yet.

But the fridge felt *empty* without them. The silence louder than usual.

He got the text just after 8 p.m.

Jordan: You good? Or just quiet?

He stared at it.

Typed, **yeah just tired**

Paused. Deleted.

Typed, **all good. Just taking it slow.**

Jordan's reply came fast:

Goddamnit, Avery, I'm coming over.

Don't ghost me.

Avery didn't respond.

Just sat on the couch, heart picking up speed.

Fifteen minutes later: knock on the door.

He opened it.

Jordan stepped in, looked around.

Noticed the notebook on the counter. The empty four-pack in the recycling bin.

Said nothing.

Just raised an eyebrow.

Avery said, "You want coffee?"

Jordan shook his head. "I want *you* to stop lying."

Silence.

"I'm not drinking," Avery said.

"Okay," Jordan said. "Define drinking."

Avery flinched.

".00 beers," he admitted.

Jordan nodded. "Cool. You've opened the door. You standing in the frame or walking through?"

Avery laughed once. "Jesus, man. Can't I breathe for a minute?"

"You can. You can't pretend you're still clean if you're halfway out the window."

Jordan sat at the kitchen table.

Avery stayed standing.

Jordan tapped the tabletop.

"Look—I'm not your sponsor. I'm not your dad. I'm not your judge. But I've *been here*, Avery. The 'not drinking but not okay' phase. It's a short hallway with a locked door at the end."

Avery looked away.

Jordan leaned forward.

"You're slipping. You're smiling less. You're not showing up. And I know that look in your eyes. It's the one I used to have the night before I relapsed."

Avery crossed his arms. Defensive.

"I haven't crossed the line."

Jordan's voice dropped.

"Then why are you arguing with someone who's on your side?"

That cracked something.

Avery sat down.

Head in his hands.

Jordan didn't say anything else.

Just waited.

Finally, Avery whispered:

"I don't want to drink."

"But?"

"But I don't want to feel like this either."

Jordan nodded slowly.

"That's the trap. You forget it gets better. And the only way to remember... is to go through it."

They sat in silence for a while.
Jordan didn't push.
He just stayed.
Long enough for Avery to remember he wasn't alone.

CHAPTER THIRTY-SIX

After Jordan left, the silence grew teeth.

Avery stood by the window, arms crossed, staring out at the parking lot.

"Why do I feel so bad?"

He opened the fridge again, out of habit.

Nothing in it but mustard, and a hazardous takeout box.

He didn't drink that night.

But he didn't sleep either.

Jordan's voice rattled in his head.

"It's a short hallway with a locked door at the end."

He hated that truth.

The next day, he skipped work.

Called in sick with a cough that didn't exist.

He walked to the corner store. Told himself it was for food.

Walked out with a bag of trail mix, a pack of gum, and a cold tallboy of craft non-alcoholic beer.

Just to hold.

Back at the apartment, he cracked it.

Drank slowly.

The *relief* hit again.

Not a buzz.

Just... space.

He wanted more space.

That night, Casey texted again.

"Round 2?"

He hesitated.

Then typed:

"You got anything stronger than wine?"

She sent back a winking emoji.

He stared at the screen.

Felt the edge shift under his feet.
Before he left, he stood by the nightstand.
Picked up the chip.
Held it.
Whispered, "I'll start over tomorrow."
Then he dropped it into the drawer.
Didn't slam it shut.
Just... walked out the door.

The bar near Casey's was loud.
Too loud.
But the noise was comforting, the faces anonymous.
He sat at the counter. Alone, for now.
Bartender: "What'll it be?"
Avery paused.
Looked down at the menu.
Then looked up and said:
"Whiskey. Neat."
The bartender nodded.
When it hit his lips, he felt nothing.
Not guilt.
Not pain.
Just... absence.
And the tiniest flicker of: **"Finally."**

CHAPTER THIRTY-SEVEN

Mouth dry, head spinning, he woke up at Casey's.

Not from booze—just from being *gone* from himself.

She was still asleep. TV still on. Crumpled tissues, two half-empty glasses, his pants inside-out on the floor.

He dressed quietly. Didn't leave a note.

Didn't want to see his reflection.

At home, he didn't shower.

Didn't eat real food.

Just stood in the kitchen, eating peanut butter with a spoon over the sink, staring at the toaster.

He opened his laptop.

Started with news.

Then porn.

Watched for over an hour without touching himself. Just... *gone*.

Detached. Numb.

Window after window.

He didn't even enjoy it.

It was noise. Distraction. White static in skin form.

When he finally shut the laptop, he felt hollow and coated in more failure than usual.

So he opened a food delivery app.

Three meals.

Pasta. Tacos. Chicken wings.

He didn't finish any of it.

Just kept eating pieces. Mouth full, throat tight, stomach bloated.

By 5 p.m., he was scrolling local casinos on his phone.

He knew it was stupid.

But stupid didn't matter anymore; he needed it.

He told himself, **"Not drinking."**

"I'm just out."
"Just playing."
He took out $400 in cash.
Walked in wearing sunglasses and a hoodie, as if shame could be hidden.
Sat at a blackjack table.
Lost $150 in eight minutes.
Moved to slots. Then roulette.
Won once—$ 50.
Felt alive for exactly seven seconds.
Then dropped it all on red. Why not?!
Red hit. Big WIN!
Red again, hope showed up on the table.
Black, it was gone.
Walked away with $11 and a plastic cup of Diet Coke.

The drive home was quiet.
Just kept whispering: **"You didn't drink."**
"You didn't drink."
"You didn't drink."

CHAPTER THIRTY-EIGHT

He didn't mean to end up at the bar.

But three days of numb chaos will make a man do strange things.

He told himself he was just out of luck. Just walking and just stretching his legs.

Then he saw the neon flicker.

Same place.

Same chairs.

Same smell of whiskey and bleach.

At the same hour, when night tries to remember it used to be day.

He pushed the door open.

The light was low. The bar was mostly empty.

Two guys are watching sports. A bartender was cleaning glasses as if she were angry at them.

He sat at the far end.

Ordered coffee.

No cream. No sugar. Just something hot and bitter to match the taste in his mouth.

He stared at the door for no reason.

Then his eyes drifted to the seat near the jukebox.

Empty.

But his brain filled it in.

The woman.

The one with the calm voice and quiet smile who said *yes, thanks for asking,* when he'd joked *"sober?"*

He hadn't remembered her name.

If she even gave it.

But her words stayed.

"You look like you're trying not to cry."

He'd wanted to say so much more that night.

He'd wanted to tell her, 'Yes, I'm broken.' Yes, I want help. Yes, I want whatever it is you've got in your bones.

But he didn't.
He couldn't find the word or the willingness.

He sipped his coffee.
Too hot.
Didn't care.

The bartender leaned over. "Need anything else?"
He shook his head.
Then—on impulse—asked: "That woman who was here before. Drinks coffee. Sits by the jukebox. You know her?"
The bartender raised an eyebrow. "Which one?"
He frowned. "She said she was sober."
The bartender tilted her head, thinking.
"Rina?"
Maybe.
"She comes in now and then. Doesn't drink. Just watches the room like she's waiting for something."
Avery felt something crack in his chest.
"Tell her... I said thanks," he said quietly.
The bartender smirked. "Sure. When she checks her messages with me, I'll tell her."
He smiled.
Didn't know why.
He finished the coffee.
Didn't stay long.
He was lost.
But maybe not as invisible today.

CHAPTER THIRTY-NINE

Misery isn't loud.

It's quiet.

It's the hum behind every breath, the weight in your limbs that makes the walk from bed to door feel like a marathon.

Depression and misery are smell-less, but they linger.

It colors the air. It coats your teeth.

It's waking up and not wanting to open your eyes because you know they'll show you the same life you're failing to survive.

Avery hadn't showered in two days.

He'd thrown out the empty food containers but not the shame that clung to them.

He'd blocked Jordan's number, just temporarily—he told himself.

He ignored emails from work.

He stopped opening the notebook.

Every minute felt like it lasted an hour.

Every hour felt like he was standing at the edge, something tall with a rope in his hand.

He went back to the bar again the next night.

Same coffee.

Same stool.

Same ache in his bones.

The bartender didn't ask questions.

Didn't need to.

The hollow behind his eyes told the story.

He sipped the coffee.

Not to feel better. To feel.

Something real.

The world: static. White noise.

Then, the door opened.

And there she was.

BRYAN WEMPEN

Rina.

Wearing a soft black jacket and jeans. Hair pulled back.

She had a coffee in hand before she even reached the bar.

She didn't see him at first.

She walked past. Sat at her usual spot by the jukebox.

And then she looked up.

Their eyes met.

Something inside Avery jolted.

Not relief.

Not excitement.

But *recognition.*

Like the universe had dropped a match into the dark and whispered:

Look around.

She walked over slowly.

Calm. Measured. Like she'd done this before.

"You again," she said.

He tried to smile. It broke on his face.

She tilted her head.

"You okay?"

He exhaled.

Shook his head.

Eyes already welling.

"No," he said. "Not even close."

She sat.

Didn't touch him.

Didn't offer clichés.

Just watched.

Waited.

He looked down at the counter.

Fists clenched.

"I'm not drinking. But I'm doing everything else. Everything awful. Everything I can to kill myself in slow motion."

His voice cracked.

"I'm so fucking tired, Rina."

130

A pause.

"I didn't know where else to go. I thought maybe—if I saw you again—I'd remember what hope looked like."

He was crying now.

Hard.

Not quiet.

Not controlled.

Sobs that shook his ribs and cracked his voice in half.

People intently stared. He didn't care.

Rina leaned forward.

Her voice was steady. Low.

"I've been there. That place where you're doing everything but putting the gun in your mouth. Because you think if you don't *technically* drink, you haven't lost."

She touched his hand, just for a second.

"You have lost. That's okay. It's what you do next that matters."

He wiped his eyes on his sleeve.

"I can't stop falling."

"You don't have to stop falling," she said. "You just have to grab something before you hit the bottom."

A long silence.

The noise of the bar faded.

Even the lights seemed softer.

Avery stared at the coffee between them.

"I'm scared."

She nodded. "Good. Means you might want to live today."

CHAPTER FORTY

It hit him while he was walking to his car.

No music.

Just Rina's voice echoing in his head:

"You have lost."

"Grab something."

He kept repeating that last part like a mantra.

Grab something. Grab something. Grab something.

He had no idea what that meant.

The parking lot was half-lit.

He reached for his keys.

Dropped them.

Bent down to pick them up and couldn't catch his breath.

It started small.

Like a hiccup in his lungs.

Then his fingers went numb.

Chest tight.

Like someone cinched a belt around his ribs and kept pulling.

He leaned against the car door.

Fumbling.

Sweating.

"Breathe, goddamn it."

His vision blurred.

His throat closed.

Avery's hands were shaking like he was freezing.

Trying to swallow, and he couldn't.

It felt like dying.

His mind screamed:

"Heart attack."

"Stroke."

"You're going to die in a parking lot alone."

The vomit just came, violently, uncontrollably.

He sank to the pavement.

Sat there.

Back against the cold metal of the door.

Palms flat to the ground, trying to stop the spinning.

No alcohol.

No pills.

Sheer panic. Terror.

The body's final alarm.

Puke — that was all his mind could process.

He started whispering.

Not praying.

Just *naming*.

"Keys. Shoes. Wind. Cold. Lights. Sky."

Something he'd read once about grounding.

Didn't help much.

But it kept him from disappearing altogether.

A car passed.

Didn't stop.

His phone buzzed in his pocket.

He ignored it.

Couldn't move.

Felt like moving would break him in half.

Then—

A shadow.

Then boots.

Then a voice.

Low. Familiar.

"Avery?"

He looked up.

It was Rina.

She knelt down. Close, but not too close.

Eyes steady. Calm.

"You're okay," she said.

He tried to answer. Couldn't.

She sat cross-legged next to him.

"You're breathing. It doesn't feel like it, but you are."

He nodded.

Tears on his face now. Silent.

"You're not crazy. You're not dying. Your body thinks the world's on fire."

Pause.

"It's trying to save you. It just doesn't know how."

Minutes passed.

Eventually the air came back.

Bit by bit.

Shaky. Ragged.

Fuck. Fuck. Fuck.

When he finally looked at her, he said, "I think I'm going to die if I don't get help."

Rina nodded.

"Good."

Then: "Let's get you to a meeting or hospital, your choice."

CHAPTER FORTY-ONE

No meeting with Rina that night.

Instead, he packed a bag.

One duffel. Jeans. A few t-shirts. The peppermints.

He hadn't touched the chip in a week.

No .00 beers.

No plans.

Just a road and the need to *be somewhere else.*

The rental cabin wasn't far. Less than two hours outside the city. Small. Cheap. Smelled like cedar and dust.

There was no TV. No Wi-Fi. Just a bed, a cracked leather armchair, and a kettle that barely worked.

Perfect.

He didn't call anyone.

Didn't text Jordan.

Didn't open social media.

He let the silence press against him like a weighted blanket.

At first, it was unbearable.

Then it became necessary.

On the second night, he sat outside on the crooked porch steps and wrote in his journal:

"I almost died in a parking lot."

"Panic lives in my chest."

"But I didn't drink."

"I wanted to."

"I wanted to crawl out of my skin and forget my own name."

"Instead, I packed a bag."

"That's not strength. But it's something."

He ate simple meals.

Oatmeal. Fruit. Toast. Nothing heavy.

Read pages of a book without finishing any of them.
Took walks without counting the steps.
Slept badly. Woke early.
Didn't drink.
Didn't lie to himself.
He didn't feel better.
But he felt *different*.
Less like a man racing toward a cliff.
More like one sitting on the edge, just watching the drop.
That felt like progress.

On the last morning, he made coffee.
No music. No distractions.
Just the steam. The silence.
And the weight of *having survived* another day.
He sipped slowly, looked out at the trees, and whispered:
"Let's try again."
Not loud.
Not sure.
But honest.

CHAPTER FORTY-TWO

Why did the apartment always smell stale these days? It was more a statement than a question.

He dropped his bag inside the door. Didn't bother unpacking.

He stood in the kitchen and let the city noise bleed through the windows.

Everything was exactly how he left it.

Which meant nothing had changed.

The voicemail icon blinked.

2 new messages.

He played them without sitting down.

Voicemail One – Jordan

"Hey. Just checking in. You're probably ignoring me, which is fair. But I meant what I said—about the short hallway and the locked door. I've got a key, Avery. I'll hold it until you're ready. No rush. Just don't disappear, man. Please."

He stood still, hand on the counter, like the voice alone might break him.

Voicemail Two – HR

"Mr. Raines, this is Carla from HR. We've received your leave documentation and want to follow up regarding your performance review and employment status. Please call us by the end of the week to avoid escalation. Thank you."

His breath caught.

"Employment status."

He'd been gone too long.

And they'd noticed.

Then—on the counter—

A letter.

Envelope torn, like he'd opened it days ago and forgotten.

Return address: **King County Family Court**

He unfolded it slowly.

Read it more times than he could count.

Past-due child support claim filed.
Nico's name was at the bottom of the document.
Filed a month ago.
Retroactive.
Five figures were owed.
$21,656.

He dropped into the kitchen chair like something pulled the bones from his legs.
No sound.
Just weight.
Grief. Shame. Fear. Anger.
They all came back. All at once.
He didn't open the fridge.
Didn't reach for anything.
Just sat there.
His heart pounded. His mouth dry. Vision tunnel-thin.
But he didn't panic.
Not this time.
He whispered, almost bitterly:
"Okay. You win."
But he didn't say it to the court.
Or HR.
Or Nico.
He said it to the silence.
To himself and to the life he'd been dodging.

CHAPTER FORTY-THREE

Up. Thirty minutes.

He didn't sleep.

Down. Awake again, forty minutes later.

On and on, all night.

Just sat in the kitchen all night, rereading the letter from the court, the messages, the blinking "NEW" on his phone.

By dawn, something in him shifted.

Not hope.

Something harder.

Maybe *willingness*.

7:32 a.m. – He called HR.

Voice shaking, palms slick, body cold.

"Hi, this is Avery. I'm... ready to talk."

He expected judgment.

Paperwork, timeframes, scheduled meetings. Consequences, but not fired.

Not yet.

"Thanks for calling back," the woman said, like it was normal.

Like his world hadn't just been collapsing for weeks.

9:17 a.m. – He texted Jordan. **"You home later? I owe you coffee. And some honesty."**

No reply yet.

But he felt lighter just sending it.

10:48 a.m. – He stood in front of the mirror.

Buttoned a clean shirt.

Brushed his teeth for the first time in three days.

Put the white chip in his pocket.

Still warm from his hand.

12:00 p.m. sharp – He walked into the AA meeting. Not the same one.

Different neighborhood. Different chairs.

Same coffee. Same knods and unspoken welcome.

He sat in the back.

Didn't wait this time.

When the floor opened, he stood.

His voice was cracked. But it was *his*.

"I'm Avery, and I'm an alcoholic."

"Hi, Avery, everyone repeated."

"I haven't been sober every day since I picked up my first chip. I told myself I was. I said it didn't count if I didn't drink. But I lied. To you. To myself. To everyone."

He paused.

Felt the silence.

"I didn't drink this weekend. I ran away. And it saved me."

A beat.

"And now I'm back."

He sat.

He didn't shake.

He just *was*.

More present.

More accountable.

Alive.

After the meeting, someone pressed a new 24-hour chip into his hand.

He almost didn't take it.

Then he did and never wanted to let it go.

CHAPTER FORTY-FOUR

They met at a quiet place Jordan liked.

No barista drama. No neon signs.

Lots of old wood, low light, and a booth in the back that smelled faintly of cinnamon for some reason.

Avery got there first.

Two coffees are already on the table.

When Jordan walked in, he paused at the door.

Then nodded.

Then walked over.

They didn't speak for a full minute.

Just sat. Drank. Let the silence settle.

Avery broke it first.

"I lied to you."

Jordan didn't flinch. "I know."

"I wanted to stop. But I wanted the comfort more."

Jordan sipped. Set the cup down.

"You almost stopped returning my texts. That's when I knew you weren't just tired. You were gone."

"I was."

Jordan nodded.

"I went to a casino. Watched porn like it was pain medicine. Ate like I was trying to fill a hole in my ribs. I didn't drink, but I wanted to. Every minute."

Jordan looked at him hard.

"You think I haven't done that exact tour?"

Avery smiled. Weakly.

Jordan leaned forward, elbows on the table.

"You did the damage. Now do the work."

Avery looked down.

"I'm trying."

"No," Jordan said, flat. "You're starting. Big difference."

Another long pause.

Avery said, "You ever think about just... disappearing?"

Jordan smiled without warmth. "Every day. Difference is, now I *tell someone* when I feel like that."

Avery nodded slowly.

"I didn't. I didn't want anyone to know how bad it got."

Jordan leaned back.

"You know what I learned? Hiding it doesn't make it go away. It only hides it from the people who could help."

Avery thought: Wow.

They drank more coffee.

It wasn't comfortable.

Yet honest.

Before they left, Avery said, "Thanks for not giving up on me."

Jordan shrugged. "I almost did. But you didn't give up either. That counts for something."

Avery stood, about to leave.

Jordan said, "What's next?"

Avery exhaled.

"Court. Nico. Try to keep my job. And me, lots of crying in a meeting tomorrow."

Jordan smirked. "Sounds like a plan."

CHAPTER FORTY-FIVE

The email.

Subject: **"Hey, Mr. R – you probably don't remember me..."**

He almost deleted it.

Then reread it.

Devon Pierce.

Junior class. Two years ago. Quiet. Smart. Wrote poetry in the backs of notebooks. Disappeared halfway through senior year.

The message was short. Rambling. The kind you only write at 2 a.m. when you're not sure if reaching out is brave or desperate.

"Think I'm in trouble. Don't know who else to contact. You used to say stuff like... the worst things are the ones we hide. So me, not hiding, I guess."

Avery stared at the screen for a long time.

Then typed back, **"Let's meet. Coffee? I'm free tomorrow."**

Devon was thinner than he remembered.

Eyes sunken, hoodie sleeves pulled down over chewed-up fingernails.

They met at a diner three blocks from campus.

Neutral ground.

Devon didn't smile.

Just sat and stirred a black coffee he wasn't drinking.

Avery let the silence breathe first.

Devon broke it.

I got kicked out of school."

Avery nodded. "Do you want to talk about it?"

"Not really. But if I don't, I might do something stupid."

The words hit hard.

Familiar.

All Avery could think was: That was me.

"Drugs?" Avery asked.

Devon gave a small nod. "Mostly benzos. Anything to keep me quiet."

"Therapy?"

"I tried. But I lied my way through it. Never liked the counselor."

Avery stared into his own coffee.

"You think I'm gonna lecture you?"

Devon looked up. "You used to."

"I was pretending I had it together back then," Avery said. "Turns out, I was drowning."

Devon blinked.

Avery took a deep breath.

"I almost drank myself to death a few months ago. Still might, if I'm not careful."

Devon looked like someone had hit him with cold water.

"You?"

"Yeah. Me."

They sat in that weird, sharp honesty for a long time.

Then Devon whispered, "I don't want to die."

Avery felt it hit deep in his chest.

"You don't have to," he said. "You just have to ask for help before it gets to the part where you stop wanting to live."

Devon nodded.

Didn't cry. Didn't smile.

Just *nodded*.

And for a moment, it felt like enough.

As they stood to leave, Avery handed him a card. Meeting list. His number is written at the top.

Devon looked at it like it weighed ten pounds.

"Will you be there?"

Avery nodded. "Yeah. I will."

CHAPTER FORTY-SIX

His first stop, HR.

The office smelled strongly of toner and cleaning supplies.

Carla was professional, but kind.

She asked about his "personal leave." He told the truth—most of it.

"I had a health issue," he said. "Mental. Emotional. Ongoing. But I'm in a program now. Getting help."

She studied him.

Then nodded.

"We appreciate your honesty. There are protocols. But there's also compassion."

He left with a plan, a last chance, and Monday appointment with the district counselor.

Second stop: Clare.

He found her in the staff lounge, grading papers with a look that said *Don't even breathe near me.*

He sat two stools down.

She didn't look up.

Then finally:

"You alive?"

"Barely."

"Good. I owe you a slap and a hug."

He half-laughed. "In that order?"

Nico called me, Avery, concerned.

He nodded.

"How about a coffee first."

Sounds good. Said Avery.

She poured slowly.

And for the first time in weeks, they talked like coworkers who had *shared silence* instead of just hallway greetings.

He didn't spill everything. He couldn't help thinking about Nico and Leo.

But he said: "I'm trying. I really am, Claire."

And Clare, without a beat, replied: "Then you're doing it right. Keep going."

That night, he called his mother.

They didn't rehash the past.

Didn't solve a thing.

But she said, "I'm glad you're still here. I am so worried, son"

And he said, "Me too."

And that was it, and enough for now.

AA meeting time.

Same room. Same burned-coffee smell. Familiar nods.

Devon was there, in the back.

Avery sat beside him.

Said nothing at first.

But when the floor opened, he stood.

Spoke slowly. Honest.

"I thought I needed to fix everything before I came back here. Turns out, I needed to come back *because* I can't fix it alone."

He sat down.

Devon looked at him sideways.

Whispered: "I'm glad you're here."

Avery smiled.

CHAPTER FORTY-SEVEN

Devon didn't show up to the meeting on Tuesday.

Or Thursday.

Avery texted twice. No reply.

By Saturday, his gut was tight. Not panic—yet—but close.

He drove by the old address listed in Devon's school file. The building looked worn, with dark windows.

He sat in the car for a full ten minutes before walking up.

Knocked.

No answer.

Then—

Footsteps.

The door creaked open.

Devon. Hoodie up. Eyes glassy.

"Avery?"

"You good?"

A beat.

Then: "No. But you can come in."

The apartment was small.

Half-unpacked boxes, a mattress on the floor, dishes in the sink.

The air smelled like weed and dirty water.

Devon slumped into a chair.

"I was clean for nine days," he said. "Then I wasn't."

Avery sat on the floor, back against the wall.

"You still breathing?"

"Sort of."

"Then you get another shot."

Devon laughed—bitter, and empty.

"You say that like it's easy."

"I say that like someone who bought a bottle just to hold it and didn't drink it but wanted to *more than anything*."

Fuck no, it's not easy, but it's possible. Said Avery.

Devon looked at him.

Really looked.

"You think I'm worth saving?"

Avery leaned forward.

"I think we all are. But more importantly, I think you don't have to save yourself alone."

We are not alone, it feels like it but we're not.

Devon blinked fast.

Eyes red.

"I don't want to go to a meeting."

"Cool," Avery said. "Then let's go get fries."

"Fries?"

"Greasy. Salted. Non-life-threatening."

Devon smiled. Just slightly.

"Okay."

They drove in silence.

No big talk. No fixing.

At the diner, over fries and milkshakes, Avery said:

"I almost died in a casino parking lot last month."

Devon stared at him.

Then whispered, "Me too. Except mine was the bathtub."

They didn't speak for a long time.

But something in the quiet felt *safe* in that moment.

Before they left, Avery pulled a folded list from his wallet.

Meeting schedule. Local therapists. Sliding scale clinics.

"Don't take it now," he said. "Just know I'll have another copy tomorrow."

Devon nodded.

Didn't say thank you.

No expectations to do so.

CHAPTER FORTY-EIGHT

2:11 a.m., the phone buzzing interrupted the quiet.

Unknown number.

Avery stared at it, chest tight.

Something told him to answer.

"Yeah?"

Silence.

Then breathing.

Then:

"Don't hang up. I don't know who else to call."

Devon.

Voice thick. Shaky. Small.

Avery sat up in bed.

"I'm here. Awake!"

"I didn't take anything," Devon said. "But I want to. It's... really loud in my head right now."

Avery turned on the lamp.

Sat on the edge of the bed.

"You safe?"

Pause.

"I put everything in the trash. But I keep looking at it."

"Where are you?"

"My place."

"I'm coming."

"No—just talk to me. Please."

Avery exhaled.

Pinched the bridge of his nose.

"Okay."

For the next hour, they talked.

About *now*.

About the pain.

The way depression wraps around the spine.

The voice that says *you're worthless* in ten different tones.

Devon cried once.

Avery didn't interrupt.

Just said: "I know that cry. I've made that sound. You're not crazy."

At 3:04, Devon asked, "Will this always feel this hard?"

Avery paused.

Then told the truth.

"Some days. But you'll get stronger. And you'll start to believe the hard days don't mean you failed."

Devon sniffed.

"Will you stay on the line?"

"Yeah."

"You tired?"

"Always," Avery said. "But I'd rather be tired with you alive."

At 3:27 a.m., the line went quiet.

Still connected.

Just breathe.

Finally, Devon whispered:

"I think I can sleep now."

Avery smiled, eyes burning.

"Good. Call me when you wake up."

"Okay."

He hung up.

Laid back down.

Stared at the ceiling.

Didn't feel like a hero.

But he felt *useful*.

And for tonight, that was more than enough.

CHAPTER FORTY-NINE

Morning sunlight cut through the blinds like a dare.

Avery hadn't slept much after the call.

But he wasn't exhausted.

He was... focused.

He grabbed coffee and drove across the city, hands steady, heart quiet in that strange way it gets after surviving a long night without breaking.

Devon's apartment was still a mess.

But Devon answered the door with color in his cheeks, hair combed back, and a bottle of water in hand.

"You didn't have to come."

"I know."

Devon stepped aside.

They didn't talk much.

Just sat on the couch, cartoons humming on the TV like background noise from childhood.

Avery handed him a new printed meeting list. Devon took it with both hands this time.

"I'm gonna try again."

Avery nodded.

"That's the job. We're not alone."

By noon, he was downtown.

Family Court.

A building that looked exactly like what it was: sterile, grim, indifferent.

He climbed the steps slowly, as if each one were a decade.

Inside, fluorescent lights. Beige walls. A line of people clutching folders and fear.

He sat alone.

Stared at the scuffed floor tiles.

Then—

"Nico Raines?"

He looked up.

Nico.

Older. Tired. Beautiful in that unfinished, real way time can't touch.

They didn't hug.

Just stared for a second.

Then Nico sat beside him.

No preamble.

Just:

"You look rough."

Avery laughed once. "I am."

A pause.

Then Nico, flat: "I'm not here to punish you."

"I know."

"I filed because I had to. Not to hurt you."

"I get it."

Another beat, a quiet moment.

Nico looked down at their hands.

"I was scared you were gone. I didn't know how bad it was until it already was."

Avery swallowed hard.

"I was scared I'd never be able to come back."

"Are you back now?"

"I'm trying."

Nico nodded. Said nothing.

That *said everything*.

They were called into mediation.

No yelling. Just paperwork. Sums owed. A slow agreement to find middle ground.

Avery didn't argue.

Didn't justify.

He just *owned it*.

When it was over, they walked outside together.

"You seeing him?" Nico asked.

Avery nodded. "Not enough. But I want to."

"We'll talk about that soon."

"Soon's okay."

As Nico turned to leave, they said, without looking:

"I don't hate you."

Avery blinked.

Then said, "I don't forgive myself yet."

CHAPTER FIFTY

What Avery called his favorite chair, more sarcastically than real, in the apartment it faced the window.

A conscious choice.

Less time staring inward. More time watching the world move and reminding himself it was still turning.

He hadn't been to a meeting in two weeks.

Didn't hate them.

Didn't crave them.

But every time someone said *"Let go and let God"*, something in him itched.

He wasn't mad at God.

There was no interest in a middleman.

He made a list.

Not "Step 8." Not church-approved.

Just names.

People.

Some in ink. Some in his bones.

People he lied to.

Used. Ignored. Disappointed.

People he loved badly.

People he didn't know he was hurting until it was far too late.

At the top: **Clare**.

Not because she was first.

Because she was *accessible*.

And because she once said, *"I owe you a slap and a hug."*

He emailed her.

Coffee again.

No awkwardness this time.

He sat across from her, put both hands flat on the table, and said:

"I'm sorry I left you to clean up the classroom mess, the parent calls, the student melt-downs. I lied and disappeared. And I don't expect you to be okay with that. But I needed to say it."

Clare looked at him.

Long and steady.

Then said, "You made it back?"

And raised her coffee in a slow, dry toast.

"To the ones who crawl home."

They both smiled at that.

Next: **his brother, Luke.**

Hadn't talked to him in over a year.

Avery hadn't shown up for their dad's memorial.

Had texted *"I can't make it"* from a barstool.

Luke answered the phone after the third ring.

Voice wary.

"Didn't expect to hear from you."

"I didn't expect to be able to call."

Silence.

Then Avery said, "I'm not looking for forgiveness. Just want to say I wasn't there. And that's on me."

I am sorry.

More silence.

Then:

"You doing okay?"

"Better. Still not great. But honest."

Luke exhaled. "Let me know if you want to talk sometime."

"I'd like that."

He didn't go to a meeting that night.

But he journaled.

And for the first time in weeks, I wrote without trying to impress or explain.

Just wrote, **"This is mine now. The grief. The damage. The recovery. The choice."**

"I'm not giving it to a higher power. I'm giving it to the version of me I want to become."

"That's enough God for today."

CHAPTER FIFTY-ONE

She wasn't a stranger.

Her name was **Eliza**. A librarian from the district office. They'd met once at a professional development day, passed jokes between bitter sips of institutional coffee.

Now she appeared again—in the corner of a bookstore Avery wandered into to avoid a craving.

She smiled. "Avery?"

He blinked, unsure if he wanted to be recognized.

But he nodded. "Yeah. Wow. You're... still in books."

She held up a novel. "Still hiding behind paper when life gets loud."

They talked.

Light at first.

Then deeper.

Something about Eliza's calm curiosity made him want to say too much.

He told her he wasn't drinking anymore.

Didn't say why.

She didn't ask.

He liked that.

It felt comfortable and weird.

They left the store together.

She offered him tea—her apartment. Just to talk.

He followed.

His chest buzzed—not with fear.

With *want*.

The kind that felt dangerous.

Not because it was wrong.

But because it *wasn't*.

Her apartment was clean, plant-filled, and smelled like bergamot.

They sat close on her couch.

Shoulders touched.

He told her about the peppermint. The chip. The casino.

Not everything.

But enough.

She listened like she wasn't trying to fix him.

Just wanted to *know* him.

And that nearly unraveled him more than any drink ever had.

At one point, her hand found his knee.

He tensed.

She noticed.

Pulled back.

"You okay?"

He didn't lie.

"I don't know how to do this without breaking it."

"This?"

"Closeness. Touch. Trust."

She nodded. "I'm not in a rush."

He exhaled.

Leaned forward.

Rested his forehead against hers.

Not a kiss.

Just contact.

His eyes burned.

But he didn't pull away.

He left that night untouched but *held*.

Didn't drink.

Didn't spiral.

Just went home with a heart that felt like it might finally want to try again.

CHAPTER FIFTY-TWO

Saturday.

The kind of day that starts with stillness and dares you to ruin it.

Avery sat in the kitchen with toast and a half-drunk coffee. The chip sat near the spoon. A physical reminder.

The first text came at 10:43 a.m.

Devon, I fucked up. I'm okay. Just. I messed up. I can't stop shaking. You around?

Avery didn't hesitate.

Where are you?

My place. Can you come?

He grabbed his keys and drove.

Devon's apartment smelled like sweat and piss; it was palpable. Eyes glassy, nose red, body twitchy in that half-detoxed way that makes you want to crawl out of your skin.

"I didn't mean to," Devon said.

"I know."

"I was scared it was working. Like... if I got better I'd have no excuse for being this person."

Avery sat on the floor.

Same wall. Same angle.

He didn't offer clichés.

Just this:

"I've relapsed too, 20 times. Doesn't mean you're broken forever. Just means you're human and hurting."

Devon cried for a long time.

It all just flowed out of him.

Avery stayed until the tremors eased.

When he left, he had two missed calls.

Nico.

Voicemail:

"I need to talk about custody, Avery. We can't delay this anymore. If you're serious about being in his life, I need to know what that looks like. We've been patient. But it's time."

He didn't call back right away.

Just parked on a side street and stared at the dashboard.

A father.

He had a son.

And the boy barely knew who he was.

Later that afternoon, he met **Eliza**.

She brought him a bag of oranges and a book she thought he'd like.

They walked. Quiet. Shoulder to shoulder.

He told her about Devon.

About the call from Nico.

She didn't give advice.

She just listened until he finally said:

"I want to be a good man. Not just a sober one."

Eliza smiled softly. "That's the right order."

They went back to her place.

He let her touch his hand.

Let her kiss his forehead.

Didn't run.

Didn't drink.

Didn't say he was fine.

That night, lying in her bed but not sleeping, he sent a text.

To Nico: I want to be a part of his life. I'll meet you. Let me know what you need from me.

Then, to Devon, proud of you. You didn't stay down; that matters a fucking a lot.

I'd say "kid," but I know you don't like that.

And finally, to himself—written on the back of a receipt in the dark:

"Today I was needed. I didn't break."

"This is the life I'm building. With both hands and heart."

CHAPTER FIFTY-THREE

Avery sat alone in the living room.

The chip in his palm. Eliza gone for the evening. Nico is still waiting for him to set a date.

Devon hadn't texted all day.

He felt the pressure building in his chest—*do something, fix it, answer the call*—but nothing felt right.

Instead, he sat.

And drifted.

Backward.

His father never left.

That would've been easier.

No, his father **stayed**—but only as a shadow.

Present in the room, absent in the heart.

A body in a recliner. A grunt behind a newspaper. A beer bottle clicking against the table like punctuation at the end of a sentence never spoken.

When Avery was seven, he brought home a drawing of a dragon.

Held it out, hopeful.

His dad struggled to look up.

Said, "That's not how fire looks."

That was it.

That was the moment.

Not trauma. Not violence.

Just the quiet death of *wanting to be seen*.

In the dark of his apartment, Avery whispered:

"I don't know how to be a dad."

And it echoed.

He looked around.

No one there to argue.

No one to offer instruction.

Just the peppermint in the bowl.
The stack of unpaid bills.
And that chip.
Later that night, he journaled.
No poetry. No insight.
Maybe the start of a little awareness.
Just this:

"He was there. And I still felt abandoned. I don't want Nico or my son to say the same about me."

"I don't need to be perfect. I need to be *present*."

"I am going to keep trying."

He texted Nico again, I'm ready. Set the time. I'll be there.
Then sat with the fear.
Didn't numb it.
Didn't run.
Just let it be part of him.
The echo of a boy still waiting to be noticed.
And a man, finally, who *notices* himself.

CHAPTER FIFTY-FOUR

So much silence, his meeting with Nico was quiet.

No lawyer.

Just two parents and one small window table at a library café.

Nico brought a notebook.

Avery brought every ounce of his nervous system.

"I don't want to fight," he said before she sat down.

"Then don't," she replied. "Just be honest."

They talked about schedules.

Boundaries.

Money.

All of it.

But the real moment came near the end, when Nico asked:

"Why now, Avery? Why are you finally here?"

He didn't look away.

"Because I don't want him to grow up waiting to feel loved."

Nico blinked fast.

Then nodded.

"That's a start."

An hour later, his phone buzzed.

It was Devon: Just left a meeting. Spoke for the first time.

I said I was scared, angry, and grateful.

I think I'm gonna go again tomorrow. You changed my life, man. Just thought you should know.

Avery read the message three times.

Then smiled so wide it hurt.

He didn't cry.

But his eyes blurred anyway.

That night, Eliza came over.

They didn't do anything significant.

Watched a dumb movie.

Made stovetop popcorn that burned a little.
He kissed her—not desperate, not afraid.
Just *there*.
She laughed into his mouth.
"You're not bad at this."
He smirked. "Still learning."

Later, they lay tangled under the blanket.
She whispered, "What's going on in that head?"
He stared at the ceiling.
Then said:
"I didn't think I'd ever get this far without destroying everything again."
"And now?"
"Now I'm scared of wanting more."
She touched his cheek.
"Wanting is good."
He nodded.
Then held her tighter.

CHAPTER FIFTY-FIVE

Three weeks sober.

And it fucking sucked.

Everyone kept asking if he was proud.

He wanted to scream: **"Proud of what? Breathing through shit and pretending it doesn't smell?"**

He hadn't been to a meeting in a week.

Hadn't journaled.

No prayers, meditation, or whatever-the-hell else was on the recovery menu.

He was doing life *dry*—and it was like walking barefoot across broken glass.

He snapped at Clare in a staff meeting.

She was making a joke about an outdated curriculum, and he just... lost it.

"Maybe if you gave a shit about the kids instead of your fucking sarcasm, they'd actually learn something."

Silence.

Wide eyes.

Clare blinked. **"Jesus, Avery**. Where the hell did that come from?"

He stormed out.

Didn't apologize.

Not yet.

Later that day, he saw his son.

Nico had arranged a coffee shop meetup.

Casual. Safe.

The boy—**Leo**—was seven.

Sharp eyes, nervous hands, hair like Avery's when he was that age.

Avery brought a comic book.

Leo barely opened it.

Just picked at the muffin and kept checking his mom.

Avery tried small talk.

Fumbled.

Sweat clung to his neck.

When Leo finally laughed at something—some dumb voice Avery made—he almost cried.

But he didn't.

Because that would feel weak.

And today, he wasn't *weak*—just angry.

At Eliza's place that night, she noticed.

"You're off tonight."

"I'm tired." Said Avery.

"You're mean."

He looked up.

"What are you talking about?" said Avery. "I don't need another fucking lecture. I'm not drinking. Isn't that enough?"

"No," she said, calm as hell. "It's not. Not if you're still acting like the man who did."

He slammed his hand on the table. Not hard. But hard enough.

She flinched.

Silence.

He backed away. Palms up.

"I didn't mean—"

"I know," she said. "But I still didn't like it."

He left.

Slammed the door.

Didn't drink.

Just drove around the city.

Angry at everyone.

Especially himself.

Later, alone, he muttered into the dark:

"Fuck sober."

"Fuck feelings."

"Fuck this version of me that can't seem to do anything right

without a beer in his hand."

But he didn't drink.

He was really struggling, ready to crawl out of his own skin.

Didn't use.

And that was the win.

Even if it tasted like blood and salt.

CHAPTER FIFTY-SIX

He both focused on and hated the way people looked at him now.

Like every step was brave.

Not drinking made him an enlightened monk.

He was still a goddamn bastard.

Just sober.

And being a sober bastard hurt *more*.

He blew up at a student.

Some kid whispered in the back row. Something stupid. Harmless.

Avery snapped.

"Do you even want to be here? You think I like teaching you this shit?"

The room went dead silent.

Clare had to cover his next class.

He didn't thank her.

Didn't talk to her.

Just left.

Eliza didn't text that night.

And he didn't text her either.

Because she'd been right.

And he didn't want to admit it.

He played three hours of poker on his phone and screamed when he lost fake money.

Screamed.

Threw the phone.

It cracked.

He left it on the floor and walked out.

Devon texted him twice.

You good?

You feel kinda... gone.

"Seriously, text me back, I am worried." Said Devon.

Avery didn't reply.

Didn't want to explain that even *his own kindness* was pissing him off now.

He visited Leo on Sunday.

The boy was quiet.

Wouldn't make eye contact.

When Avery asked him if he wanted to hang out next weekend, the boy just shrugged.

Shrugged.

Avery felt like something splintered.

Later, in the car, he punched the steering wheel until his knuckles bled.

And still—still—he didn't drink.

He didn't go to a meeting either.

Didn't meditate.

Didn't call Jordan.

He just sat in the car, bleeding and breathing; he hated both.

At home, he picked up the peppermint again.

Looked in the mirror and muttered:

"You're still broken."

"You just stopped bleeding on people."

"Burning the place down."

Then, finally, he cracked.

He pulled out his journal and wrote:

"I hate everyone who says this gets better."

"Because if it does, I'm doing it wrong. Life is a lie."

CHAPTER FIFTY-SEVEN

Avery didn't show up for work.

Didn't call in.

Just… didn't go.

No one came knocking.

The phone buzzed twelve times that day.

Clare.

HR.

Devon.

Eliza.

Even Jordan.

He let them all go to voicemail.

Didn't open a single message.

Didn't want to explain what he couldn't put into words.

He felt like a failure even while sober, that the silence was louder than the chaos had ever been.

Avery wanted help but couldn't stand being *seen*.

He was alone.

He didn't eat.

Didn't sleep.

Just paced. Laid on the floor.

Watched dust in the light like a movie.

Stared at the ceiling and wondered how long it would take for someone to notice if he just stopped being.

At one point, he whispered, "I'm fine," to the empty apartment. By midnight, the peppermint was in his mouth.

The chip was in his hand.

But they felt like props in a play he no longer wanted to watch.

He finally checked his phone.

A text from Eliza:

"You don't have to be okay. You have to be reachable."

He stared at it until the screen went black.

Didn't answer.

At 3:12 a.m., he finally stood up.
Not because he wanted to.
Because his legs were cramping.
He opened the fridge.
Stared at nothing.
Closed it.
Sat on the floor again.
Pulled the blanket over his shoulders.
Whispered:
"Please."
To no one.
To everything.

CHAPTER FIFTY-EIGHT

No memory of falling asleep.

He woke up with his face flat on the floor.

Wood grain versus the usual tile pressed against his mouth.

Back aching.

Phone buzzing somewhere across the room.

He didn't move.

Didn't want to.

Didn't care.

There was a menagerie of smells in the room.

Dirty clothes, sweat, and old coffee.

He hadn't showered in four days.

Hadn't eaten in two.

He stared at the wall until the light changed and his stomach cramped from emptiness.

Even then, he didn't get up.

No breath deep enough.

No thought that didn't turn on him.

He was a canary in his own coal mine.

The only sound was the hum of the fridge.

A quiet little fuck-you from the universe:

Look, something in here still works.

Eventually, he crawled to the couch.

Pulled a blanket over his head like a cave.

He wanted to sleep forever.

To disappear.

To call someone.

To scream.

To drink.

The chip was on the coffee table.

He stared at it like it was a dare.

He didn't feel strong.

Didn't feel anything.

He whispered, "I can't do this," but even his own voice sounded fake.

He checked his phone.

Ninety-two missed messages.

He scrolled.

Eliza:

"Please. I don't need you to talk. Just let me know you're alive."

Jordan:

"You don't owe me anything. But don't do this alone."

Devon:

"Hey. I get it. I really get it. But if you die, I'll never forgive myself for not saying I love you, man."

That broke something.

His fingers shook as he hit the call button.

Jordan answered in one ring.

"Avery?"

Avery tried to speak.

Nothing came out.

Then a single word:

"Help."

Jordan didn't ask questions.

"Okay. I'm coming."

Thirty minutes later, Jordan was at the door.

Avery couldn't stand up to open it.

Jordan let himself in.

Sat beside him on the floor.

No sermon.

No lecture.

Just *presence*.

"I don't want to die," Avery croaked. "But I don't know how to live either."

Jordan nodded.

"I know."

"I didn't drink."

"I know."

"I wanted to."

"I know."

They sat there.

Shoulder to shoulder.

But Avery wasn't alone anymore.

And that was something.

Not everything.

But something.

He closed his eyes.

And for the first time in days, he slept.

CHAPTER FIFTY-NINE

I need space, that is what he told Eliza.

Told Jordan he was going to Santa Fe.

No one knew the real reason; it was simpler:

He didn't want to be watched when he broke down again.

The drive was short. Uneventful.

He dropped his bag, sat on the edge of the bed, and stared at the minibar like it was a blinking cursor on an empty page.

He didn't open it.

It dared him to be "a man."

He walked the streets that first day.

Ate enchiladas that tasted like a distant memory.

Saw the adobe buildings, the dry sky, the artists.

Tried to feel something.

Failed horribly.

That night, he made it past dinner.

Past the bar downstairs.

Back to the room.

He stood in the shower, letting the water pound his back, trying to feel relief.

Tried journaling.

Wrote:

"Don't do it. You know what happens."

Then added underneath:

"But maybe this time you'll stop before it's too late."

He opened the minibar.

Stared at the tiny bottles.

Picked one up.

Spun it in his fingers.

Set it back down.

Paced the room.

Called no one.
Then—
He drank.

No fanfare.
Just a long sip of whiskey that burned less than he remembered.
And that *felt worse* because of it.
Then a second.
Then two more.

He didn't blackout.
Didn't rage.
Didn't call anyone or punch mirrors.
He just lay on the bed, half-drunk, half-numb, empty.
The ceiling fan spun slowly overhead.
The bottle rolled to the carpet.

In the morning, he woke up sick but not shocked.
Looked in the mirror and whispered:
"You knew exactly what you were doing."
And somehow that hurt more than the hangover.

He didn't check out early.
Didn't pray. Didn't care.
Bag packed, tip left, he walked out like a man leaving a crime he
knew he'd commit again.
Avery's only thought: he would.

CHAPTER SIXTY

Wandering, lost, definitely chasing something.

He rolled into the parking lot.

Didn't text anyone.

Eliza had messaged:

"Home safe?"

He left it unread.

Jordan called twice.

He silenced it.

Devon wrote:

"Still here if you need me."

He blocked the number.

The apartment was exactly as he left it.

He dropped his bag by the door and lay down on the floor like it had been waiting for him.

Didn't change.

Didn't shower.

Didn't unpack.

He moved through the week like his own skin didn't fit.

Work, mostly.

Words, few.

His coworkers stayed away.

They knew better.

That's what he wanted.

That's what was killing him.

The loneliness — sharp, palpable.

At night, he bought more bottles.

Different liquor stores, so no one noticed.

He wasn't bingeing.

Not yet.

Just enough to dull the panic.

Take the edge off the silence.
Slow the thoughts.

Eliza came by once.
Knocked.
Waited.
Left a bag of food on the handle.
He watched her leave through the peephole and still didn't open the door.
Didn't even reheat the food.
Just threw it away the next day, untouched.

He told himself this was a phase.
That he just needed time.
That he was *thinking*.
But thinking started to feel like drowning in molasses.
Every hour heavier than the last.

He stopped checking his email.
Ignored a call from HR.
Missed a payment on his car.
He started sleeping through entire weekends.
Woke with the taste of whiskey and bile in his mouth, whispering:
"This is what you deserve. You piece of shit."

And still—still—he didn't call for help.
Didn't go to a meeting.
Didn't tell anyone the truth.
Because this time?
He meant to disappear and finish what he had started.

CHAPTER SIXTY-ONE

It arrived on Tuesday.

Late morning.

He hadn't checked his email in days.

Hadn't planned to.

But he needed something from the district portal—an old document, a calendar.

And there it was.

Subject: **"Administrative Review Notice – Immediate Response Required"**

His stomach dropped, but not with fear.

With *acceptance*.

He already knew.

He'd missed classes.

Dodged calls.

Rotating subs and disoriented aides had covered his students.

He hadn't submitted grades.

Hadn't responded to Clare.

Hadn't shown up for a scheduled IEP meeting with a parent who'd waited thirty minutes in the front office.

The letter was cold.

Precise.

They'd be reviewing his **conduct**, his **unexplained absences**, and his **professional reliability**.

He sat at the desk, trying to read the second page.

Eyes blurry. Head pulsing.

He didn't feel angry.

Didn't blame.

He felt like someone watching his own life shrink in a rearview mirror.

At noon, he got a call from **Carla in HR**.

He answered.

"Mr. Raines, we've left multiple voicemails—"

"I know," he said.

Silence.

Then, gently:

"We're required to notify the licensing board if this isn't resolved in a formal hearing. I don't want to do that, Avery."

He nodded to himself.

"I'm... sorry."

"Are you okay?" she asked.

That question.

He almost laughed.

"No."

Another pause.

"I can connect you."

"I know. No need. I'll be fine."

He hung up.

Closed the laptop.

Stared at the wall.

Whispered:

"Well... there goes that."

Didn't rage.

No breakdown.

Just opened the cupboard, found the last bottle.

Poured two fingers into a coffee mug.

Didn't drink it right away.

Just held it.

Then whispered:

"This is what you wanted, right?"

"My best effort got me to the bottom."

Avery heard that in an AA meeting.

DRINK: SOME FIGHTS ARE WORTH THE SCARS

But he didn't drink it.
He left it there.
Untouched.
Sat in the chair until the sun went down.
Alone with the one thing he hated more than anything.
Himself.

CHAPTER SIXTY-TWO

The plan was to sit, not drink; it was never that.

To feel something awful and leave the bottle untouched like some fucked-up victory.

But the moment he stepped into the bar, the cold air, the hum of some modern jazz, the clink of ice in a glass, his brain said: **"We're home. You will feel better soon."**

And that was it.

He sat in a dim, private corner booth.

Didn't hesitate.

"Whiskey. Double."

No chase.

No guilt.

Just the warmth of destruction crawling back into his bones.

The first sip was holy.

Not because it healed anything.

But because it was erased.

Pain. Guilt. Identity.

All gone.

Just liquid, burning, and forgetting.

The bartender dropped off his second drink with a low whistle. "Rough night?" the man asked, wiping down the bar absently.

Avery didn't look up. "Something like that."

"Well," the bartender said, giving him a once-over, "you look like you walked in here with a whole lotta baggage."

He smirked. "If you come back, that's your nickname now—**Bags**."

Avery let out the closest thing to a laugh he could manage.

"Never had a nickname," he said, voice a little hoarse. "Not once. But if I come back…" he paused, eyes flicking up, "I'll take it. Seems only fitting."

He was two drinks in when the phone buzzed.

Devon.

Avery almost let it ring out.

But something in his gut twisted.

He answered.

"Dev."

Pause.

"You okay?" Devon asked.

"Me? Yeah," Avery said, voice thick. "Golden. Fucking thriving."

Silence.

"You sound drunk."

"Sharp ears, kid."

"Where are you?"

"Where do you think?"

"Avery…"

"I know."

Another long pause.

Then Devon, softer:

"I was gonna tell you I made it two weeks today."

Avery's chest caved a little.

He looked down at the half-finished glass and felt everything and nothing at all.

"I'm proud of you," he slurred.

"You don't sound proud of yourself."

"I'm not."

More silence.

Devon's voice cracked:

"I can come get you."

Avery laughed. Bitter.

"Tables turned, huh?"

"Yeah," Devon whispered. "But I meant it when I said I love you, man. You're one of the reasons I'm still here."

Avery closed his eyes.

"Don't say that," he said, thick with tears. "Not tonight."

"Why?"

"Because I'm not the reason I'm still here."

He hung up.

Didn't finish the drink.

Didn't stay.

Just left.

Walked the night alone.

Didn't know where he was going.

Only knew he couldn't go back to being anyone's hero.

Not tonight.

Not like this.

CHAPTER SIXTY-THREE

Avery sat on the curb outside another bar.

Head in hands. He had his elbows on his knees.

The cold of the concrete seeped into his spine.

He hadn't thrown up.

Hadn't passed out.

He was just... still.

Heavy.

Blank.

The glass of whiskey felt a thousand years away and *five minutes too recent*.

Headlights pulled up slowly.

He didn't look up.

Door shut.

Footsteps.

A cracked voice:

"You alive?"

Avery laughed into his hands.

Devon. Jordan. Standing over him.

Of course.

"The fuck are you doing here?"

"GPS."

"Jesus."

"You weren't answering. I didn't know if you were gonna—"

"I didn't."

Devon stood in front of him. Arms crossed. Nervous. Pale.

But there.

Still there.

"I don't want help," Avery muttered.

"Didn't come to help. I came to sit."

A pause.

Then Devon lowered himself to the ground next to Avery on the curb.

Jordan sat next.

The silence was thick.

Avery finally said, "I'm not who you think I am."

Devon nodded. "Me neither."

They sat there a long time.

Cars passed.

Laughter from the bar door behind them.

The world kept spinning.

Avery's stomach churned. His brain fogged.

They just sat there.

Didn't judge.

Devon said:

"You helped me when I was half-dead."

Avery groaned. "And look at me now. Slurring in the fucking gutter."

"You're not in the gutter."

"Feels like it."

"You're just on the curb."

"Semantics."

Avery chuckled.

"My new nickname is BAGS; it seems fitting, doesn't it?"

Then he choked on it.

Then cried.

Worked his way into uncontrollable sobbing.

Just a quiet collapse behind his eyes.

Salt on skin.

Devon stayed silent.

Hand on Avery's shoulder. Lightly letting him know he wasn't alone.

After a while, Jordan said, "We don't have to go to a meeting."

"I don't want God in my face tonight."

"Neither do I."

"Then what the fuck are we supposed to do?"

Jordan looked at him.

"Stay alive, for another night, man."

Avery nodded.

"Okay."

And for the first time in weeks, his words didn't feel like a lie.

CHAPTER SIXTY-FOUR

Morning light peeked through the blinds.

Devon sat on the couch with a notebook on his lap.

Avery nursed a hangover and an overwhelming sense of **not being dead**, which was somehow worse and better than he expected.

"So," Devon said, "we suck at this alone."

Avery raised his hand in a half-assed agreement.

Devon kept going.

"So what if we try a thing?"

"A plan?"

"Like... not a twelve-step thing. Just a stay-alive, do n't-drink, do n't-ghost-each-other thing."

"We check in daily. We don't lie. If we fuck up, we tell each other. And if one of us disappears again, the other one *shows up*."

Avery stared at the ceiling.

Then back at Devon.

"You sure you wanna bet on a guy who drank whiskey out of a coffee mug three nights ago?"

Devon smiled. "You sure you wanna bet on a guy who was detoxing in a bathtub last month?"

Touché.

They wrote it out on the back of a grocery receipt.

The Deal:
- Daily check-in.
- One honest feeling a day.
- No disappearing.
- No savior shit.
- No judgment.
- Stay alive.

"We do whatever it takes to beat this thing."

They both signed it.

Devon folded it and put it in his wallet.

That afternoon, Avery got a text.

Nico.

"Can we talk?"

He stared at it for a long time.

Then answered.

"Yes. When?"

They met in the park.

Nico came alone.

Avery could tell from her walk that she already knew *something*.

Maybe Eliza had said something.

Maybe HR.

Maybe **Leo had picked up the smell in his breath** and said nothing.

She sat.

Didn't smile.

Didn't attack.

Just said matter-of-fact:

"You are drinking again?"

He didn't lie.

"Yes."

"For how long?"

"A week. Maybe two. I stopped again yesterday."

She looked away.

Said nothing.

Then finally:

"I can't have Leo around you if this is what's happening."

"I know."

"I'm not angry, Avery. But I don't trust you."

He nodded.

"I don't either."

They sat in silence for a while.

Then Nico said, "I want him to know you. But only if you're someone he can depend on. You don't have to be perfect. Just *present*. Sober. *Safe*."

Avery swallowed hard.

"I'm working on it. This time, not alone."

She looked at him then. Really looked.

"Leo deserves that."

"So do you."

Before she left, she handed him something.

A photo.

Leo in his Halloween costume.

A little pirate with a plastic sword.

"Keep it," she said.

CHAPTER SIXTY-FIVE

The first sign came on a Tuesday.

A missed call from Devon.

Then another.

Then nothing.

Avery texted.

No response.

He called.

Voicemail.

All day.

All night.

Nothing.

Wednesday morning.

Avery paced his apartment like a man waiting for a storm to make landfall.

He scrolled through old messages.

Looked at the pact.

Read the words.

"Stay alive."

It felt like a fucking joke.

By afternoon, Avery drove to Devon's place.

He banged on the door.

No answer.

He texted again.

You okay? Say anything. Please.

Then finally—

At 3:42 p.m., his phone buzzed.

Devon:

"Don't come in. I'm not proud of this."

Avery didn't reply.

He walked around the back.

Climbed the rickety stairs to the old balcony. Checked the sliding glass door.

Unlocked.

He let himself in.

The smell hit first.

Booze. Sweat. Vomit.

Devon was curled up on the couch. Eyes half-open. Skin pale. Lips cracked.

Empty vodka bottle on the floor, another half-full on the table. No food in sight.

Avery froze.

His mouth went dry.

Then, slowly:

"Dev."

Devon didn't move.

Didn't look at him.

Just mumbled, "I broke it. I broke the pact."

Avery knelt beside him.

"You're not dead."

Devon finally turned his head, tears wetting the corner of his cheek.

"Maybe I should be."

Avery gripped the side of the couch like it could anchor him.

"Don't you fucking say that."

"You thought it too," Devon whispered.

Avery's voice cracked:

"Yeah. I did. And I didn't. Because you called me. You sat next to me. You showed the fuck up."

Devon blinked slowly, the world moving at half-speed.

Avery grabbed a trash can, wiped his mouth, got himself water, and stayed close.

"Hospital?" he asked.

Devon shook his head. "Not yet."

"Okay. Okay. Then we ride this out together."

The next six hours blurred.

Avery never left his side.

Kept the lights low. Kept the TV on.

At one point Devon whispered:

"Are you gonna hate me now?"

Avery stared at him, hollow-eyed.

"No, man. I'm gonna hate what this disease keeps trying to do to us. And I'm gonna stay."

At 2:13 a.m., Devon finally slept.

Avery sat in the chair beside him, exhausted and alert and sick with fear.

He stared out the window.

Into the dark.

And whispered:

"Don't leave me too."

Avery forgot about himself for a few hours.

CHAPTER SIXTY-SIX

Avery calmly called 911 at 3:06 a.m.

Devon wasn't unconscious.

But he wasn't lucid either.

Mumbled half-sentences.

Shivered under the blanket.

Breathe shallow.

Avery didn't wait for it to get worse.

He made the call.

The EMTs arrived in under ten minutes.

Avery answered questions with a voice that was like sandpaper and steel.

Yes, he drank.

Yes, he's detoxing.

Yes, he's been struggling.

Yes, I'm his emergency contact.

That last part surprised them.

But Avery didn't flinch.

Just nodded and climbed into the ambulance like he'd been training for it all his life.

At the hospital, it was bright, slow, and awful.

They took blood. Hooked up fluids and monitored his vitals.

Avery didn't sit.

He stood beside the bed like a guard dog.

When a nurse asked if he was family, he just said:

"Yes."

At 8:47 a.m., his phone buzzed.

Unknown number.

He answered.

It was HR.

Cool voice. Legal phrases.

The decision had been made.

They had "reached a threshold of inaction that could no longer be sustained."

Effective immediately.

The district no longer employs Avery Sloan.

He said nothing.

Just listened.

Nodded to no one.

And hung up.

He looked at Devon, who was finally sleeping.

IV in his arm. Face pale. But breathing.

Alive.

Avery sank into the chair beside him.

Pressed his hands together.

Whispered:

"You better fucking make it through this."

"Because I just gave up everything I had left to stay here."

A nurse came in and offered him a cup of coffee.

He took it.

Burned his tongue, again.

Watched the slow beep of the heart monitor.

One beat at a time.

One minute at a time.

This wasn't the life he planned.

But it was the one he **chose**.

And that, somehow, felt like **beginning again**.

CHAPTER SIXTY-SEVEN

She texted him at noon.

"Can we talk today? No pressure. I'll come to you."

He stared at it for a long time.

Then finally:

"Not now, maybe tomorrow if you want."

She came by with a soft knock.

He opened the door. It looked worse than she remembered.

But cleaner than she feared.

Eyes tired.

No alcohol in the air.

Just a man stripped to his truth.

They sat in the kitchen. No distractions.

Just the space between two people who'd almost been something.

Eliza started.

"I've been thinking about this for a while."

Avery nodded.

Didn't interrupt.

"I care about you. I really do."

"I know."

"But I can't hold this with you."

He looked down.

"I don't want you to."

"I hoped it would get easier."

"It didn't."

"No." Said Avery.

She let the silence stretch.

Then reached across the table. Touched his hand.

Not a promise. Not a goodbye kiss.

Just... *human contact.*

"You're not unlovable, Avery."

"You just need to love yourself before anyone else can stay."

He swallowed. Hard.

"I'm sorry," he whispered.

Her smile was small, sad, and honest.

"I know."

"I watch hummingbirds sometimes. They look crazy, but they're in control. Just thought I'd share something normal."

Eliza frowned at the odd timing, then softened. "No, I didn't know. I like them too."

She stood.

He didn't follow her to the door.

She turned, one last time.

"If you ever get better… if you ever feel even a little whole — write me. Not for us. So that I'll know you made it."

He nodded.

She smiled, eyes bright with tears.

The door clicked shut.

And Avery sat still for a long, long time.

Not broken.

Not angry.

Just… alone.

But somehow, for the first time in days, the silence didn't feel like punishment.

CHAPTER SIXTY-EIGHT

It took him a week to build the courage to write the email. He rewrote it nine times, maybe more.

In the end, it was just simple:

"Hi Nico,

I'd like to see Leo again. When you feel I am ready. I'm not asking for anything big—just a walk. I'm trying. For real this time. Let me show you, not just make promises.

—Avery"

He hit send.

Then immediately stood up and walked away from the laptop.

Didn't want to wait for the reply or obsessed on the answer.

He made a list.

Not for therapy.

For *survival.*

Small things I can do today:

1. Shower.
2. Make a resume.
3. Apply for one job—even if it sucks.
4. Drink water.
5. Text Devon a meme, say hi to Jordan.
6. Don't ghost.

He taped the list to the fridge and snapped a picture.

The job hunting was brutal.

No teaching license anymore.

No schools would touch him.

He looked at warehouse work.

Delivery driving.

Assistant positions.

He even thought about making sandwiches.

For once, the pride didn't scream.

It just muttered, 'Do what you need to do.'

At 1:43 p.m., Nico replied.
"I appreciate you reaching out.
Leo's asked about you a couple of times.
We could meet for an hour this weekend.
Let's keep it light. A walk sounds okay."
Avery reread the message three times.

He walked to a nearby café and filled out a paper application.
The manager was kind.
Didn't ask about the gap in employment.
Said they'd be in touch.
He thanked them twice, awkwardly.
Avery submitted another application — this time at a restaurant in Santa Fe called Snaggle Dumpling, which was located a couple of doors down from Counter Culture, a popular spot in town. He'd found the opening online. It looked like a cool place and needed a server right away. He figured he couldn't afford the rent up north, but he didn't want to miss the opportunity.
Got some things crossed off the list.
Back home, he crossed every item off the fridge list.
Even texted Devon a photo of a pigeon with wild eyes holding a frying pan.
Devon replied, "Accurate depiction of my brain right now."
"You okay today?"
Avery typed, **"Not great. Not dying though."**
Then added, **"Moving. Just a little."**

That night, he didn't drink.
Didn't journal either.
Just sat by the window and breathed.
Watched the streetlights blink on.
And whispered:
"One honest day."

CHAPTER SIXTY-NINE

It was early afternoon.

Nico picked the park.

Very public. No pressure.

Leo had a juice box and a toy dinosaur.

Avery had clean clothes and no idea what the hell he was supposed to say.

"Hi," Leo said. Not cold. Not warm. Just seven.

Avery knelt. "Hey, bud."

Nico stood off to the side but close enough to hear.

The silence was thick with memories.

They walked the trail—wood chips crunching under sneakers.

Leo told him about a field trip.

About a spider in his classroom.

About how juice boxes aren't as cool as Capri Suns, but *whatever.*

Avery listened.

They shrieked together, watching a roadrunner and a lizard race around the path.

He didn't say much about himself.

Didn't talk about Eliza.

Or the hospital.

Or how the sound of a bottle cap still made his hands sweat.

He just asked questions.

Simple ones.

"Still into dinosaurs?"

"Still not like math?"

Leo nodded.

Avery breathed.

They sat on a bench near the duck pond.

Leo climbed the back of it like a jungle gym.

Nico watched. Quiet. Arms folded.

She finally said, "You look better."

He didn't answer.

Then, "I'm not drinking today."

She nodded.

"I can tell."

More silence.

But it wasn't choking this time.

Just *full and some happiness.*

"I'm not gonna make promises I can't keep," Avery said.

"I don't need promises," Nico replied. "I need proof."

He looked at Leo.

Saw his face in that kid's half-smile.

Felt it split him open.

"I'll be here," he said. "Every time you let me."

When the visit ended, Leo hugged him quickly and ran ahead.

Nico didn't smile, but her voice softened.

"Same time next week?"

Avery swallowed the lump in his throat.

He walked home alone.

Didn't stop at a bar.

Didn't open a bottle.

Just walked. Dry. Quiet. Thinking.

He was sober.

And maybe, for now, that was enough.

CHAPTER SEVENTY

Later that night, Avery sat on the floor.

Back against the couch. Lights off.

Peppermint in one hand. The photo of Leo in the other.

"You're a piece of shit."

The voice in his head, sharp and sudden.

He nodded.

"You failed him."

A breath.

"He'll forgive you. You'll only break it again."

"I know," he whispered.

Then another voice. Quieter.

The one he almost forgot he had.

"But you love him."

Avery looked at the picture.

Leo, holding a plastic sword, half-smiling like he didn't know how much weight his existence carried.

"I love you," Avery said out loud. Voice shaking.

"I fucking love you more than I know how to be okay."

The voice came back.

"That's not enough."

But Avery fought it.

"I don't need it to be enough forever. I need it to be enough *today*."

He pictured Leo's face.

The way he talked about bugs.

The juice box. The dinosaur.

The way he hugged him like it didn't have to mean anything—but it still did.

And for the first time in weeks, Avery didn't think about drinking.

Being the guy Leo could call when he was heartbroken, or scared, or proud.

"I love him more than I hate myself."

He repeated it.

Louder.

Like a spell.

"I love him more than I hate myself."

And the craving quieted.

Just a little.

CHAPTER SEVENTY-ONE

It was taped to the door.

"FINAL NOTICE – 72 HOURS TO VACATE" on finalizing white paper. Red print. No room for negotiation.

He just stood there and whispered, **"Of course."**

The job rejection came that same morning.

He opened the email out of habit, still holding on to hope.

"We appreciate your interest in our café team. After reviewing your application, we've decided to pursue other candidates."

He laughed.

It wasn't funny.

But the timing was *hilarious.*

He texted Devon, "Want to flip a coin for which one of us has the bigger shitstorm this week?"

Devon replied a minute later, "Only if you let me call tails. It feels appropriate."

"You good?"

Avery packed a box.

Just one.

Photos. Books. Journal. Leo's drawings.

He didn't have much else that mattered.

He spent the afternoon calling shelters. Programs. Friends, he hadn't ghosted. Found a temp gig unloading supply trucks—3 a.m. shifts, four days a week.

It wouldn't cover rent.

But it might cover **a room**. A mattress.

Somewhere.

That night, he met Nico and Leo at the park again, before work.

DRINK: SOME FIGHTS ARE WORTH THE SCARS

Leo ran ahead.
Avery walked more slowly.
He told Nico the truth.
Eviction.
Temporary job.
Still dry.
She didn't hug him.
But she said, "Thanks for telling me."

Later, Leo gave him a drawing.
It was them—on a hill, under a lopsided sun.
Stick figures holding hands.
He didn't say anything.
Just folded it, carefully, and slipped it into his coat pocket.

Back home, Avery stared at the boxes, and the empty shelves.
Said aloud:
"You're not done."
"Not yet."

CHAPTER SEVENTY-TWO

A worn structure wedged between a gas station and a bail bond office.

Faded siding. Broken porch lights. A whole symphony of problems.

But it came with a paycheck.

And a **unit with a door**.

Estrada Luxury Apartments is the next step.

Avery signed the paperwork in an office that smelled like mildew and opportunity.

The woman behind the desk said, "We just need someone who can answer phones and not steal copper wire or sell meth."

He nodded. "I'm qualified for that."

They gave him a key.

Unit 3C.

Upstairs. No working heater. Carpet that felt like cardboard.

But it was his place.

He dropped the single moving box on the floor.

Sat down on it.

And just breathed.

Outside the sliding glass door, a dog barked nonstop.

Inside, it was quiet enough to hear himself think.

He almost missed the chaos.

Almost missed the ache of rock bottom.

Because this, it was *in between*.

Later that night, he found a bar down the street.

He didn't go in.

Just stared at it from across the parking lot.

The lights were warm.

The drinks were cheap.

He stood there for a full five minutes.

Hands in his pockets.
Mind at war.
Then he turned around.
Walked home.
Opened a can of soda water.
And whispered:
"Not tonight."

He taped Leo's drawing to the wall above the mattress.
Set a peppermint on the windowsill.
Sat in the quiet and made peace with it—for now.
He wasn't drinking.
He wasn't okay.
He wasn't done.
But he had a door to lock.
And a key.
And a reason to wake up.
He was trying.

[THE END – BOOK ONE, DRINK.]

October 11, 2025.

ABOUT THE AUTHOR

Bryan Wempen is an author and entrepreneur living in Santa Fe, New Mexico, who writes about grit, recovery, and the messy beauty of the human spirit. With many years of experience in sober recovery, he brings raw honesty and compassion to his storytelling, whether in short stories, memoirs, or fiction.

His earlier work includes a nonfiction title such as **"Sober Is Better** which is a deeply personal reflection grounded in sharing his lived experience with getting sober. In fiction, he explores themes of power, ambition, and suspense with his first cozy country murder mystery, a political thriller, and, more recently, with **"Adoption, Inc.: A Family Affair,"** a dark comedic love story. It's a character-driven novel rooted in American contradictions and set in New Mexico.

Bryan's voice blends candid reflection with dark humor. He writes about deeply flawed characters and fractured families, always in search of truth, serenity, and redemption in quiet, unexpected moments.

When he's not writing, he's cheering on his favorite English League football team, questioning BBC mystery story lines, reading new and old fiction, or hiking and riding in the high desert around **Santa Fe** with his wife, Michella—a modern tinwork artist.

He has embraced the New Mexico debate of the merits of red versus green chile and, on occasion, enjoys a mild, buttery cigar while chatting with a mate, and pondering his next set of stories.

ACKNOWLEDGMENTS

"As the world spirals into greater complexity, with annihilation and bondage looming for many, I offer my wishes, prayers, and meditations for the return of balance, kindness, and for humanity to remember the wisdom hidden in both its wounds and triumphs."

B Wemper

www.ingramcontent.com/pod-product-compliance
Lightning Source LLC
Chambersburg PA
CBHW031334170626
46807CB00002B/696